CAPSULE STORIES

Masthead

Natasha Lioe, Founder
Carolina VonKampen, Publisher and Editor in Chief
Claire Taylor, Editor
BEE LB, Reader
Aimee Brooks, Reader
Stephanie Coley, Reader
Rhea Dhanbhoora, Reader
Hannah Fortna, Reader
Teya Hollier, Reader
Mel Lake, Reader
Kendra Nuttall, Reader
Rachel Skelton, Reader
Deanne Sleet, Reader
Annie Powell Stone, Reader
Emily Uduwana, Reader
Amy Wang, Reader

Cover art by Darius Serebrova
Book design by Carolina VonKampen

Paperback ISBN: 978-1-953958-16-7
Ebook ISBN: 978-1-953958-17-4

CAPSULE STORIES

Autumn 2022 Edition

Falling Leaves

Contents

Falling
Leaves

As you walk home, the leaves swirl around your feet, crunching beneath your shoes with each step. Reds, oranges, yellows, and browns color the street so vibrantly that you stop and take a photo. For a brief moment, you want to send her the photo, to share this beauty with her, and then you remember that she's gone. You put your phone back in your jacket pocket and shuffle down the sidewalk, lost in memories. You don't look up until you're home. The big oak tree in the front yard welcomes you, its yellow-sleeved branches rustling in the wind and waving hello.

The oak is dying. The arborist said it wouldn't last much longer and that he would come back before spring to cut it down. You agreed and set up the appointment, though the thought of losing the tree stung your eyes with tears. The oak shades half the house, dapples the wood floors with patterned sunlight in the late afternoon, covers the sky in a canopy of green half the year, blankets the ground in color each fall. It's part of your home, a constant in your life, the way you tell the seasons. Its whispering branches lull you to sleep each night. But the oak, too, will leave you sooner than you'd expected— at least you have time to say goodbye.

You make a cup of tea and sit on the window seat in the living room facing the oak. A squirrel scurries up the thick trunk to some unseen hiding place to store its food for the winter. Does it know the tree is dying, that its days are numbered? Next year, the front yard will look empty without the oak. Maybe you'll plant a new tree, full of hope and promise. But for now, you're content to sit and watch the tree unclench its tight fists and let go, golden leaves floating from tree to ground.

The End of Summer

Anna Kibbey

She breaks one night in
September, scatters fountains
on our scorched eyelids

her ragged laughter
overhead, diamonds spilled
across morning lawns

diminuendo
that single, long-held chord can
still blush apple cheeks

yields such sweetness in
her decay, the sealed jam jars
in memory of quince

of sun-drunk plums splashed
on sheets, innards mined by wasps
like forensic drones

October conducts
its chaos of leaves, bronzing
on mist's eiderdown

hollow, beneath it,
she's sleeping more, doesn't eat,
yet the slip of her

holds on so fiercely,
her fingers rake deep furrows
as she leaves, the turn

almost a relief,
that nothing, no one, dies as
beautifully as her.

nothing,

no one,

dies as

beautifully

as her

Feuilles d'automne

Mary McColley

When the berries turned orange, I turned gray
        though my hair still summer-blonde, still twisting gilt
        in summer-light (no alchemy succeeds)
Wore my soul on my heels, ran and ran
        in shadows, past trees' river-doubles
        (rippling, shuddering selves)
Scraped my fingers on bark to feel something,
        grew my hair long and bound it in knots
        atop my skull (crown of split endings,
        forked like snake-tongues)
I coughed like I could spit out my heart
        but there was only fall's phlegm within me.

Fall

Mary McColley

Ducks spear the water—
The leaves have lost their pretense of green,
   they die as we all do, individually
The spines, the stems snap beneath the soles of shoes,
   flicker in wind over green beer bottles
smashed into gems,
   I walk the canal, I tread the corpses—
Dust from dust to dust again.

Hometown, or Trees

Mary McColley

Here are the trunks and the roots and the twigs,
the beeches pines oak maple, leaves that burn
away the summer every fall, leave themselves
on the ground, cinder and husk.
I used to gather up the dead
with green-wire rake and listen
to their brown susurrus of regret.
Here are the enchanted grasping limbs.
We always cut them back,
pick acorns like nits from the hair of the grass.
Wintercome, I shiver by
the orange smear of their bones alight
and all the next days, chimney bricks
keep burning with hardwood heat. Here
are the woods. Gray brown and cold.
Here are the hearts and the spines,
that break sometimes beneath the snow
and in springtime, bloom again.

Down Down Down

Mary McColley

A cold wind blew for two days and
I called it happiness, the cold,
let my skin shiver into white blanks,
the beds of my nails set with ten purple dusks
each curving crescent clenched tight in pockets.
Clouds fled the sky, lots of
frail leaves couldn't hold to the trees any longer, they
crumpled, skidded down the sidewalks like me.
Tendrils of clover curled under a bench.
Children chased dying white seeds through the wind
and all birds that daubed the chimney tops
were black. I sat among the grass and knuckles, the grasping weeds,
pulled my shoulders back tight beneath my sweater:
blade to sharpen narrow blade,
to fly in gray wind and blow me away.

Gray Day

Paul Hostovsky

It's the almost that I love
about a gray day
like today. In weather
like this, I almost
feel a kind of joy:
the heavy sky, the feeling
in the air of imminent release.
I feel like I could almost
cry. Cry as I haven't
since I was a boy.
Because I haven't let myself.
The overcast sky says *almost*.
The charged air says *could*.
You could do this.
You could let yourself go,
feel the thunderous sobs,
wave after wave, shoulders
heaving, lungs emptying
in that jagged way
that almost looks like
laughter. And the hiccuping
like a child that comes after.
It could feel so good,
says this feeling in the air.
Almost like joy, says the sky.

Ashes

Sam Neboschizkij

Elsie knew that eventually she would have to get up. The telephone would ring, or her sciatica would act up, or she'd have to use the bathroom. But for now, she sat silently at the kitchen table, head resting on her hands. Particles of dust drifted along a shaft of late-afternoon sunlight, diffused by the sheer curtains that provided only the pretense of privacy. Though the leaves were no longer green, the air remained heavy: a lingering summer's last dance.

She closed her eyes, hoping for a moment of rest, but in the darkness, she felt everything more acutely. The tap dripped rhythmically, punctuating the ticking of the old clock above the stove. There was a pressure building around her, a sense that the walls were inching closer, the ceiling hanging lower. She shifted her stockinged feet so they were flat on the linoleum. Now at least she wouldn't float away.

Elsie grimaced, a pain shooting down her left leg.

"Okay, okay," she conceded to no one in particular, pushing herself up from the table with a heavy sigh. She needed a cup of tea; yes, that would make the difference. It was the only thing she could think to do at a moment like this. As she waited for the kettle to boil, she picked a white hair from her black dress and thought about Henry.

He hadn't been a particularly large man, but what he lacked in stature he made up for in bravado. He walked with his chest puffed out, as if he had just sucked the air from a balloon, and resented anything that disrupted his progress, from stoplights to grocery lines. He laughed as loudly as he shouted, and he did the latter far more often than the former.

When they had met, she was a young eighteen, and he her twenty-five-year-old tutor. When he slipped his hand between her knees during an algebra lesson, she felt a stirring in her breast. Now, it was thirty-six years later, and if wings had once fluttered, they had long since been clipped.

The kettle whistled, and Elsie poured herself a cup. She stirred in some honey and was about to sit back down at the table when she paused. Holding the saucer carefully in both hands, she instead walked into the living room. It was a shabby space, or perhaps cozy, if one were feeling generous. The wallpaper, once swirling with golden geraniums, was now a lifeless tan and torn in several places. The carpet was dense with years of living—subsumed by dust, sweat, and thousands upon thousands of paces. In front of the television was Henry's recliner, his shape perpetually carved into its cushions. Aside from work, this was where he had spent most of his time. There was also a small loveseat in the room, which looked almost as new as the day they had bought it. Back then, she still believed in the possibility of romance; now, the ill-named couch was nothing but a taunting reminder of how naïve she had been.

Henry had been an unsuccessful insurance salesman and Elsie his stay-at-home wife. She had always desired, and a few times offered, to get a part-time job to improve their situation, but Henry was dead set against it. He didn't want her getting any ideas, he said, though he never specified what kind of ideas he meant. He was a man who eyed everyone with a mix of suspicion and envy, and he would rather continue on barely making ends meet than ever have to wonder where his wife was, or worse, with whom.

Elsie sat down on the loveseat, sipping her tea. The TV was angled away from her, facing Henry's armchair. She picked up the remote and carefully selected the power button. A soccer match flickered to life. As she began flipping through the channels, a shameful pleasure washed over her.

It was a Monday afternoon, and she was watching television. This was what it felt like to do nothing. This was what it was like to not be needed.

Almost as soon as the thought entered her mind, she felt a twist in her stomach. She glanced away from the television at the small wooden box she had left by the door when she returned home that morning. She hadn't yet found a permanent place for it, and the guilt swiftly overwhelmed her. She turned off the television—stupid, wasteful thing.

A shrill ring pierced through her thoughts. She hurried to the kitchen.

"Hello?" she said hopefully, picking up the phone.

"Elsie! I'm so glad I caught you. Is this a bad time?" an older woman shouted.

Elsie held the receiver farther from her ear. A sigh almost crept out, but she caught herself in time.

"Hello, Lorraine. No, it's alright."

"I just wanted to call to see how you were doing, with Henry and everything, since we missed you last week. Oh, how *terrible* it must be for you."

"Thank you."

"Because he wasn't really that old, was he? None of us at church could believe it when we heard," Lorraine prattled on. "Even though we'd never met Henry ourselves, just seen him when he came to pick you up, but *still*, it was quite a shock to us all."

"Yes, it's been difficult."

"Oh, I'm sure, I'm sure!" Lorraine cried, with such a flair that Elsie suspected she might be enjoying herself. "But you know what they say," she continued, assuming a confidential tone, "blessed are those who mourn."

Elsie clenched the phone a little tighter.

"Will we see you on Sunday then?"

"I'm sure you will," Elsie replied.

"Oh, good. It will do you wonders."

"Yes," said Elsie. "See you then."

Elsie hung up the phone. She was still for a moment, unsure what to do next. Normally, she would be starting on Henry's dinner, marinating the meat, peeling the potatoes. But she didn't feel particularly hungry, and anyway, she had never liked meat or potatoes herself. What if she made something different tonight, something to her own liking? A butternut soup perhaps, with sage? Or with rosemary sprigs and a dash of black pepper? Outside, a car horn blared, and Elsie jumped and brought her palm to her heart. Instinctively, she glanced toward the front door, where she could just see the wooden box. The soup was a silly idea, she chastised herself. Fresh sage, how extravagant, really.

Elsie's hand trembled as she pushed her hair behind her ear. She felt ridiculous just standing there, like a guest who had arrived too early and was waiting to be told what to do.

Forgetting that she was still wearing her outdoor dress, she went to the cupboard and took out her rubber gloves. She began by scrubbing the counters, though they were already quite clean, then moved on to dusting the spice jars, and finally to mopping the floor. In the living room, she wiped down every bottle of Henry's liquor collection and had started to tackle the carpet when the vacuum gave out with a groan. The sudden silence surprised her, and she stopped where she stood, feeling the sensations of her body return: the pain radiating down her thighs to her calves, the sweat trickling from her temples, the ache at the back of her neck.

She looked out the window and saw that a blue evening had fallen, dull and transitory like a cold bath about to be drained. Her gaze traveled across the curtains to the photographs that hung in a row on the wall—in need of dusting, she noticed. Taking care not to knock them askew, she ran her rag along their edges, one by one.

There was her wedding portrait with Henry, both of them wearing big smiles, though Henry's did not extend to his eyes. He had just had an argument with the photographer, she remembered, where he accused him of paying too much attention to the bride. Then there was Henry's mother, round faced and serious, who had died before Elsie and Henry had met. "She was a saint," Henry used to say, "too good for this earth." And finally, there was Renee: Renee as a baby, her mouth bursting with laughter that Elsie could almost still hear; Renee as a young girl, holding her father's hand, both squinting into the sunlight; and Renee's graduation photo, where she gripped her diploma with pride and perhaps something else? Elsie took the photo from the wall and held it closer, examining it. There was an expression on her daughter's face that unnerved her, and she was reminded of an image she had once seen of a woman who had just been rescued from the sea.

Elsie stared at the picture for a long time before wiping the dust from its glass and replacing it on its hook. Then she went to the kitchen, picked up the phone, and dialed. The line rang and rang. Finally, the answering machine clicked on.

"You've reached Renee. Leave a message, and I'll get back to you as soon as I can."

A beep sounded. Elsie hesitated.

"Hi, Renee, it's your mother. I wanted to let you know that I picked up your father's remains today." She ran her finger along the spotless counter. "I know you said you didn't want to hear from us, but I thought it was important to tell you, just so . . . well, just so you'd know."

She closed her eyes. "I miss you, Renee. Talk soon."

Elsie winced as she hung up the phone. It was the wrong thing; she always said the wrong thing. She could feel the memories bubbling up, the sounds growing clearer as they rushed toward the surface: dishes smashing, doors slamming, a man's slurred shouts, a girl's terrified screams. But what was worse was what she couldn't hear—her own voice rising strong and defiant—because the past was unforgiving, and where her voice should have been, there was nothing but a cowering void.

Elsie opened her eyes and shook her head, willing the sounds to sink back to the depths where she had long ago left them to rust. She suddenly longed for Henry's barking voice to fill the house so she could put on a smile and fetch him a drink and escape from herself into him. But Henry was not there, and the echoes were growing louder.

On the counter was an old radio, rarely used. A poor man's television, Henry had called it. Desperately, she rotated the dial until a rousing piano concerto burst through. But it was not enough, so she turned it up, and up, until she could hear nothing else.

She hadn't realized she was moving until she was steps away from the little table where all that was left of Henry lay. All his strength, all his threats, the fear he felt and the fear he inspired, relegated to this tiny wooden box. She picked it up, feeling its insignificant weight in her hands, and for the first time since Henry died, she knew exactly what to do.

The toilet's flush was drowned out by the piano's frenzied cries.

In the bedroom, she unzipped her dress and let it fall to the floor before climbing into bed. She lay on her side, limbs folded into herself, trying her best to think of nothing. The day's light, but not its heat, had faded, leaving the room suspended in a stifling, leaden gray.

The music came in waves. First, she felt the bass rumbling in her stomach, then the highs tingling up her spine, until her every nerve was filled with vibration and her body began to expand. Elsie turned onto her back as her arms and legs loosened, stretching, reaching, until she had spread herself as far as she could go. *This is all of me*, she thought. *This is all I am.*

It was a long time before she stopped crying, but when she did, she fell into a deep and dreamless sleep from which she didn't wake until morning.

Empty
Spaces

Nancy Huggett

You ask how I spend my time.
In calendaring, I say,
in childcare, chores, and laundry,
but secretly in covert corners poeting.
I gather words like autumn leaves.
Rake them into piles, into paper bags to hold them.
Then read that it's best to leave
the leaves for moles and microbes, toads and shrews,
to nestle through the cold.
I spread my words
along the ground. Shake
them out and let the mice, or God or goodness,
bury down and burrow
into the empty spaces I have left
to warm you in the wintering that comes.

To the
Woods

Katherine D. Perry

---

for Ralph Waldo Emerson

I went to the woods
with a borrowed dog
and walked where horses made wide trails
over fallen pine and oak trunks,
and I thought of you in your Massachusetts cabin,
your mother washing your clothes,
so you could follow the tree branches
away from the Industrial Revolution.

I left chicken bones slow cooking
in carrots, onions, and garlic
because I'm tired of wasting leftovers,
and I'm searching for ways to escape
the technological revolution
and the global pandemic
and the everyday chores
of taking care of children.

Here under canopy,
I ask the trees to help me.
A single leaf, red and glowing in the November air,
falls into my graying hair
and pulls saltwater from my eyes,
washing away what separates me
from the forest.

I don't have to come here for this,
but I keep forgetting what was sacrificed,
how far we've pushed so that we can survive
when we leave Earth for the next planet.

I will wander here in your memory
until all the leaves fall,
until my own hair stops growing.

washing   away
what separates me
from   the   forest

September's End

Ann Weil

after "Maypole" by Lucia Perillo

Clear-eyed skies, cider smiles, calico leaves
crunch underfoot. All perfect, save the quilt
of black-eyed Susans—a disheveled bed,
gold crowns browned, stalks kneeling as if to pray.
Yet—if the bed is a constellation,
and Fall its telescope, the faded blooms
are lonesome stars in need of a cricket's
song. Or say the bed is a leaky boat,
then the Susans are its crew, yearning for
the safety of shore. Or say the bed is
a fresh grave, the brittle stems are bones of
the dead, not yet willing to be buried.
As we are not yet ready for shrouded
skies, ebbing light, and Winter's lonely wait.

This Life

Eve Croskery

The ocean is different in autumn.
The sun rises later, dazzling displays of
apricot smudged skies that we witness
bundled in jackets and blankets.

There's a chill in the air,
cheeks bright and flushed,
the dragon fog of our breath,
numb toes racing through
sharp and biting sand.

I look around me—
this life I once hoped for,
our son climbing rocks with
a newfound confidence,

our daughter tottering on
wobbly legs—so ready to soar.
Each stage is fleeting,
I have learned that now.

Today, they squeal and holler
at the thrill of the waves
racing up the sand to catch them.
My son declares, *I love you,*

I love you, I love you before bed.
My daughter finally finds her feet
and takes her first determined steps
away from me.

The Season for Sowing

Eve Croskery

We feel the change of season, the heat sucked from the air. Colors morphing, life slowing. Our vegetable patch has reached the end of her summer splendor. The last crimson tomatoes plucked and devoured, the vines now spent and withered. Planting gives us something to look forward to, to feel the rhythm of the earth in our bodies. My son and I climb within the bird nets, a packet of seeds clutched in his small hot hand. By winter, we will gather snow peas, hanging—slender and bright—from the climbing tendrils. Last year, his dimpled toddler fingers still fumbled with the shells; we curled together as I cracked them open and passed him each shining pea, which he crammed into his mouth. Now, he helps me make tiny holes in the soil, places a seed in each, gently pats it down. We wait. As the fresh shoots emerge and reach skyward, this version of him will have quietly grown into something new. Here I am, constantly letting go of one season while marveling at the next unfolding in front of me.

Shorter Days

Mary Clements Fisher

I dangle by a thread, like the faded crimson and gold leaves withering on the grapevine on the edge of my garden. I pluck one grape and pop it into my mouth. I roll the seeds from cheek to cheek and spit them out. The taste of purple lingers on my tongue. I drank purple with a man—I've forgotten his name but not the passion we shared—in front of a blazing blue and ocher fire on an autumn afternoon when I knew who I was.

He held me close when I felt cold. I held him until his last breath. His eyes never left mine until he went still and white. My windows rattled with thunder and muffled my cries the first night alone. He's never returned. Now shadows swallow his name and face. I shudder and shake off the chill of such muddled midnight memories.

Bask in the moment says the second summer sun. Dusky days lie ahead, so I obey and wallow in her warmth. Her morning rays wake me with a kiss. My mottled, tanned arms prove my love affair with her, and her midday heat paints my cheeks tawny peach. I dread sundown and the winds of winter. They paint my lips and fingertips ice blue. This afternoon's midday heat caresses me from head to toe.

A lizard tickles my ankle. After last night's long-awaited rain, she dries at my feet. She blinks. *Trust the cycles of the seasons.* I warn her about an early frost tomorrow. Lizards drop from trees in warmer climes when a cold snap surprises them. Raining lizards. A chill crawls up my spine. My reptilian friend must burrow deep before her blood runs cold. I refuse to be buried underground.

Who did I ask to sprinkle my ashes on the beach at sunrise? A child whose amber hair shines and swings as she walks. I gave her life in a snowstorm and suckled her on the shortest days and longest nights. Her summer spirit bloomed and filled my autumn and winter days until she grew up and moved away. She comes back. She's not gone forever. Her name dawns on me—Aurora. Sunshine breaks through the fog of forgetting. I'm a mother. This is who I am.

I breathe deeply. A mix of sweet hay and muck rises from soaked paddocks beyond three gnarled trees with balding heads. Apples cling to their branches, out of reach of the horses' stomping and whinnying for a treat. The children who ride them must be in school. I pick my way around gopher holes and through grasping grasses to the fence. One gray bay filly flicks her mane. Her velvet nose nudges my hand. *Ride with me through fields of poppies and seas of needlegrass. Let the billowing winds lift you up.* I shiver with the thrill of jumping ditches as a young warrior woman, unafraid of falling, failing. Our wild eyes meet. This is who I was.

A strange woman with cloudy eyes in a wrinkled mask stared back at me in the mirror this morning. A dimple buried in sunken cheeks reminded me of Mama. I went to call her, to ask her if she knew this woman in my house, but I couldn't find my phone. Where did it go? I had no idea. My to-do list on my blackboard called my attention. Number one on the list: pick whatever's left in the garden. I remember where the garden is. Under my feet. Solid, unmovable. But things disappear. Things decay.

Abandoned raspberry stalks and dried-up strawberry plants, zucchini's moldy leaves, stems like mummified arms, offer their regrets. A bee sips from fading coneflowers and black-eyed Susans and buzzes past my ear. *Time to rest. Celebrate your last harvest.*

Hurrah for peachy roses, quince, coreopsis blooming butter. Thyme, rosemary, and basil flourish despite my neglect. Hurrah for purslane, crabgrass, buckhorn, discarded gopher traps, for diligent diggers of dirt mountains—survivors in this holy place of in between.

The wind picks up. The horses paw the ground to hail me, a warrior at rest on my wobbly bench. I pull the man's sweater around my bent shoulders and head toward home with a violet sunset complimenting the leaves swirling around my feet. I'll build a roaring fire, sip ruby wine, and dream of my love and me wrapped in warm embraces. This is who I want to be again.

The North
Garden

Susan Alexander

It was summer when you left me
at home and alone.
Autumn surprises your return.
The earth has abandoned you.

I planted too late in the season.
See, only three pods on the scarlet runner.
Its leaves have already dropped.

The yellow bush beans are naked,
stems bent over stunted fruit.
The kale for our winter harvest
turned red and brown. And these lush
tomatoes that held such promise
are mourning women, hair hanging down.
Their green burdens will never ripen now.

I am silent to your homecoming.
Blood knows how to pool inside,
protect the heart. My hands
are too cold to touch.

You point to snow peas that love the chill.
Crowded with blossoms and tender
sweet pods, they offer everything
to the last evening sun.

Dust

Susan Alexander

He wants to talk facts: where will I live,
what about a dog, shouldn't I begin decluttering
the cupboards? I beckon him to the window,
to see the big leaf maples at the beach,
solid gold before the day shuts down.

He doesn't move. There's a kind of glow
around him too when he sleeps for hours
in the mornings and afternoons. I want to do
nothing and watch him. He sees me and I drift
above the mountain across the sound.

When we thought he was fading quickly,
he demanded I go,
find a new life.
We were just married,
safe in those embroidered folds.

What is unspoken gathers like dust
in rooms never swept. Where does it come from?
I have nicked his books about endings.
Who are they for? He won't read them.
I scan for treasure maps inside.

I want to remember how often I argue and how often
he is right and warm on our bed, his laughter
when I tell him my favorite mistakes of the day.
His pale body rises to dress and drive away;
I cherish these missings, my practice rounds.

We live with this dust. I lack belief
in dogs and downsizing. I long to carry
his light under my skin. I can't help
but wonder, what's in store without a soul
to laugh when I am ridiculous and every leaf fled.

and

every

leaf

fled

How to Let Go

Mona Anderson

The wind whispers *it's time*
and without protest
leaves let go of lives hung
in green splendor and shared sky

begin farewell journeys
like their ancestors, breathe
the embrace of spruce and pine
blanket tender roses, merge with ponds

ride the wind upward like runaway kites
float above fields before they light
join friends raked in piles for squeals and dives
crunched under careless feet,

silent in their descent
graceful in death's long breath
that begins in oak, maple, birch
ends hereafter in the earth.

October Arrival

Jodie Duffy

I woke to a whisper in my ear   *today*

downstairs the dog looks at me, whines softly
I cannot settle.   A restlessness
itches in my core
our feet pace in circles

a daddy longlegs drifts through the living room

the tree outside the window
is laden, its branches hang
heavy

I know you are coming.

red squashed berries
bleed on the doormat

a gust of wind presses on the walls
I rock back and forth on my birth ball
in front of the TV

I don't make a cup of tea

I stand at the window
until my body moves me on

I brace myself against the next gust of wind
this time it rattles at the door

are you getting closer?

the afternoon folds into the evening
wrapped in the dusk, I focus inward

from here on, the nights get longer

but in the darkness, together
we will nest, together
we will grow

the tree

outside

the window

is laden

its

branches

hang heavy

Mother Tree

Cynthia Landesberg

Fall descends simultaneously in both of my hometowns. Though separated by half of a planet, they sit just a few degrees from each other on those imaginary latitude lines that connect East and West. When the calendar turns to September, residents of Washington, DC, and Busan, South Korea, yearn for a hint of fall crispness, but the sticky summer heat simmers on. It is not until October that the Northern Hemisphere tilts just far enough from the sun to usher in cooler air, a message to the leaves that it is time to let go, to sacrifice for the mother tree so it can survive the cold, dry winter. And it is the leaves' protest, their defiant delay, that results in an eruption of color, a brazen final gasp of life before loss.

And so it was in the fall of 1983, when my adoptive Jewish family in the suburbs of Washington, DC, and my biological Korean family in Busan, South Korea, experienced this autumnal blend of hope and loss that changed all of our lives. I cannot be sure how it happened, but this is how I imagine it.

Washington, DC, United States

Rosh Hashanah came early that year, the Jewish New Year that oscillates between early and late September, tradition refusing to bend to the modern calendar. My adoptive family, New York transplants chasing the stability of a federal job, moves around the kitchen in their townhouse, a new suburban sprawl community built on cow patties and accessible via a recently expanded two-lane farm road.

"Apples and honey on Rosh Hashanah," my six-year-old sister sings, her brown curly hair bouncing as she skips around the kitchen, waiting for my parents to put out the treat. The family of three sits down at the table, my sister's legs kicking wildly, always in motion.

"L'shana tovah!" My sister yells the New Year greeting, and my parents smile, enamored by her enthusiasm, in love with her charm.

Busan, South Korea
I spend my last weeks in the womb of my birth mother, Omma, inching around like a sloth as I orient myself downward in my ever-shrinking home, nature's eviction process. I am coaxed to sleep by the rhythm of Omma's swaying cadence as she walks along a concrete road, carrying an open umbrella, not to protect her from rain or sun, but from shame.

The sizzling heat entraps the fetid smell of fish in the air as Omma walks past her parents' home, recalling their last conversation months ago. "How will you feed a baby? How will you care for one? How could this happen?" Omma places her right hand on me reassuringly, to calm me from the torrent of thoughts she is sure I can hear.

Washington, DC, United States
The leaves still show green, and the heat lathers thick onto the polyester black stockings my sister wears to synagogue for Yom Kippur. The joy of Rosh Hashanah has been replaced with the somber contemplative tone of its dark twin. My mother is hungry, fasting to repent for her sins, and her emptiness reminds her of the deep hollowness where a child should be. She thinks about adopting domestically again, but she waited so many years for my sister, and she wants to be sated fast. As she raises and lowers her body along the dark wooden pews in unison with her congregation, she prays for another child, for a filling to her emptiness, for satisfaction in the new year.

Busan, South Korea

Omma is feeling full now, her appetite low and her pregnant belly stretched hard. The mid-September humidity feels heavy, an extra weight on her already overburdened hips. Her stomach tightens and loosens, like a runner before the big race. She knows it is happening soon.

The owner of the fish stand fired her months ago, as soon as she could no longer pass off her bloated body as simple weight gain. She never liked working there anyway—the always wet bucket she sat on as she scaled Pacific mackerel, the tiny slices on her fingers from when she let her mind wander, and, of course, seeing *him* every day. He said he loved her. He said he would take care of her. His parents told him no. He obeyed.

So, instead, she stands in line each day for daily wages at the SamHwa factory, a factory that produces the same New Balance sneakers that my adoptive father wears. No one at the factory cares that she's pregnant. They do not care about the noxious fumes she inhales. They only care about the money that comes with providing products to America. Omma inspects the rubber soles as they chug down the assembly line, not realizing she is carrying another export good in her womb.

Washington, DC, United States

The sun cuts across the sky earlier now, arguing with the humid summer heat, laying out its case for the leaves to let go. My parents watch my sister leap like a frog as they sit in mismatched metal framed lawn chairs with plaid plastic weaving, the kind that frays and peels and sticks to your bare legs.

"I got the application from the adoption agency I told you about," my mom says.

Silence. They already had a fight about this. He told her he did not want to adopt again. He told her that their family of three was enough. He silently worried their marriage could not withstand another child. He lost.

"It's on the desk. Will you fill out your part?"

Silence.

"Hello?" she prods.

"I hear you," he says, his lungs like two clamped balloons, releasing just enough air to say those words and then closing again, holding in the frustration, anger, and fear of not being heard, of the inevitable loss of what they already have.

Busan, South Korea

As the first fall breeze weaves around the globe to Korea, Omma's contractions are undeniable now. She crouches on the floor of the room she rents from a widowed ajumma, who does not ask questions in exchange for help around the house. Hearing Omma's moans, the ajumma slides open the door and silently sits with her, knowing every new life needs a witness. Omma succumbs to the pressure, the twisting, the violence in her body, and she gathers all the sorrow and pain and worry and joy and pushes it all out with me. A vibrant burst of hope swells over her as she looks down at me, in awe of my realness, my solidness, the fact she is no longer alone.

Washington, DC, United States

The minute by minute decrease of sunlight each night has finally triggered the chlorophyll in the leaves to taper, revealing an onslaught of fiery color, a radiant showing of perseverance before the end. My mom completes the adoption application and my dad begrudgingly writes a check for the thirty-dollar fee, and they send her hopes and his reluctance

---

in an envelope to an adoption agency. Their application that states "We enjoy and love children and would like a second child" is read by a social worker who smiles and puts their application on the teetering pile on her desk. There are so many families who enjoy and love children, and the social worker will answer their prayers.

Busan, South Korea

The sea salt grips on a chariot of whipping wind, rocking the red and orange leaves as they cling to their branches, determined to stay. My tiny hands pull at Omma's breast, but nothing is coming out. Omma worries as I start to doze without eating again, conserving energy, my body still not much bigger than when I was born.

"Meokja," she says with forced sweetness, encouraging me to eat. I try, but her body refuses to feed me. Omma pushes my head harder to her breast with one hand and squeezes herself like a cow with the other, tears welling, head thrown back in desperation. This is our last gasp, our last chance to stay together. We've almost made it seven weeks.

Washington, DC, United States

The leaves begin to give in to the inevitable forces larger than them, and their fight has begun to drain from their faces. My father walks to the community mailbox, key gripped in his chilled hand. He sees a letter from the adoption agency. Dread hits him again.

"We are pleased to inform you that your application for adoption has been received. Please remit the half of the home study fee: $425," it reads.

He refolds it and wanders back to the house. When he shows the letter to my mom, she smiles.

"It's really going to happen," she says, looking at a commanding oak tree, still with dynamic red and orange leaves.

"It's really going to happen," he mumbles, staring at the tree next to it, already bare. Much like the leaves on that tree, he has accepted his fate.

Busan, South Korea

On the other side of the world, Omma has given up too. She has been overpowered by the forces of a rapidly industrializing country, by a society that looks down on women like her, and by a government that promotes international adoption as a public relief program paid by Westerners. She walks quickly amid the dried maple leaves dancing on their pointed toes in the wind, their swirling and tapping cloaking her in anonymity. The crescent moonlight casts a mellow beacon on the house she chose the week before, the house with the woman who always takes an early morning walk, the house where I would be found.

She arrives outside the gate and walks toward the low stone wall with tall wooden double doors. A miniature roof hangs above with a steep A-frame adorned with beams shaped like cake rolls, slate gray and painted long ago. Omma adjusts a quilt around me so it tucks under my chin and gently touches my closed eyelids with her lips. The thud and clank of a man pushing a cart startles her, and she freezes until he passes. She must hurry. She holds me close to her and whispers a blessing, a blessing that lives in me as wordless longing and constant searching. She lowers me to the ground, detangling my fingers from her hair for the last time. A whooshing gust loosens the last leaves on the trees and sweeps her away.

With no name or birth date left, the woman in the house calls the police, who declare I am abandoned and pass me to an adoption agency. I am placed on a train to Seoul the next day, destined for an orphanage then foster home. I leave Busan behind with nothing but the enduring feeling of loss each autumn.

Washington, DC, United States

A few weeks later, my sister skips through the door, jacket peeling off her arms, a few crunchy leaves trailing behind her. She clutches the envelope my family has been anticipating for weeks, the one with their child in it. They anxiously open it and stare at my face—round and large with a broad forehead and cherub cheeks, my dark eyes like pinpricks staring right back at them. And in an instant, Omma's daughter becomes theirs. My parents look up from the picture and out of their screen door to a line of bare dogwood trees shivering naked, steeled for the winter to come. The leaves have all fallen, sacrificed to save their mother tree, just like me.

Assimilation

Emerald Liu

In autumn we shed our tongues
as maple leaves
our mute words
float to the floor
to form a tapestry
        our feet will trample into
                    dust
                        we sweep out of the house
                            to forget our heritage

Mid-Autumn

Emerald Liu

Leaves throw crisp confetti
to celebrate
paving the street in honeycomb colors
with each step
delicious auditory sounds delicate as Murano glassware
accompany my walk to the Asian supermarket
tradition coats the air the way
caramel ceremoniously glazes enamel
giving away childhood secrets hidden in cavities
Eyeing up the aisles, scanning down each shelf
my fingers read the textures of boxes and packages
eagerly watching out for Wing Wah's signature mooncake
I feel my tongue curl as a cat's tail around its owner's leg
when remembering the taste of lotus paste
At home my father slices through its thick, tender crust
revealing generational memories
dense, sweet filling
the void of my grandmother's laugh
temporarily relieved
with each bite

Parting

Emerald Liu

Parting a mandarin
I unfold in unison as the six segments bloom open
and unfurl across the formica surface of the table
the morning after
another goodbye
the sunlight is swallowed by the mist
converting color to grayscale
when I think about your luminescence
there's a lump in my throat
which I try to carry in the palm of my hand
      foraging
            hiccups
      as wild brambles
      dropped carelessly
between the earth and orange
of fresh fallen leaves

Deer Visits

Jennifer Clark

---

for my mother

The white-tailed doe comes mostly at night. My mother lets her in through the sliding glass door, watches as gangly legs cross gingerly from snow or spongy grass into her living room, so unlike her grandchildren who leap fearlessly across thresholds.

The deer curls on her husband's end of the couch. She sits on her side, so close she can smell acorn and the deer's apple breath. They watch The Weather Channel. Usually she tells the deer about her day, the way the sun spun shadows on the kitchen counter or how she tried to recall the sound of her husband's laugh. Sometimes they both fall asleep.

On nights she finds herself alone—the deer visiting the old man across the road or the couple around the corner—she opens her husband's closet, though she's trying to do this less often, troubled that his forest smell is fading.

She tells this to the doe who is a good listener and licks her tears. When the deer leaves, my mother returns to her side of the couch and reaches out, pressing palm to the warmth of where deer has been.

Dear Tree Committee

Jennifer Clark

My mother is my mother isn't my mother today.
I tell you this only because I mistook your arborist
for a black tupelo tree when pulling into the driveway,
having returned from taking her for a CT scan, and there
he was, standing still as a sapling beneath the sprawling
silver maple, the one that shrugs a shaw of brittle branches
at night, whose belly you sprayed with a big orange X.

He waved me over, and his fingernails—the color of dark bark—
swept the sky. He spoke beautifully of trees, made me forget
that out west roads buckle and cables melt as the heat here
messes with my mother's head.

Your arborist said trees, with their canopy of leafy hair,
can cool air as much as ten degrees, that our tall friends,
rooted to earth longer than us, decide what limbs
they must let go to survive.

Don't let go, my mother said to the X-ray tech
who lowered her head.
Don't cut down this tree, I told the arborist.
Why is letting go so hard?

Listen to the tree, he said, pulling out a rubber mallet
and tapping the maple like the doctor tapped my mother's knees.
The tree sang, a rich baritone of timbre leaves.
Listen again, he said and tapped the opposite side.
A hollow gasp escaped.
Tell me, how can two songs be in one tree?

Tomorrow will bring more debris. Much like the maple,
my mother, known for her adaptability, flashes a silvery underside
and is letting parts of herself go—first, it was my father's clothes,
then all the good dishes. Though growing frail, she holds firm
to her mother branch and frets over grown children.

We will miss how the flowers transform
to winged seeds in summer.

she holds

firm to her

mother

branch

Try to Remember

Emma Thom

Virginia May was in the habit of forgetting things, much like her mother. She'd left her keys in a patient's room a few days ago, and this morning she found Charlotte's hair bow in the cabinet with the wine glasses. The things she forgot were small, but enough to leave some worry as she left the hospital.

She let the radio scan as she drove away from the city and past the empty quarry, nearing her parents' home. The clouds rolled slowly overhead, covering half of the sky with an ominous blue gray. The other half was feathered with clean, white clouds and the bright rays of the sun. It looked as if the light was chasing the dark. Or maybe the dark was chasing the light. She could see a storm was coming. For most of her life she'd loved the crackling sound of thunder and the smell when the rain touched the warm asphalt. She'd sit with her mother and father and watch as lightning struck the emptiness of the field behind their house. But in the last few years, the noise began to bother her mother, who retreated to her bedroom while Virginia and her father watched the water trickle down the windows and onto the ground.

Virginia had been let off work early to be with her mother, so she drove with a loaf of bread and a carton of soy milk in the passenger seat. The fake milk sloshed in its container as the tires rumbled over the gravel that led into her neighborhood. Her mother was lactose intolerant, but she had probably forgotten that too.

The leaves on the sugar maples had become a mass of color, tangerine shades layered with maroon and yellow, like an enormous marigold in full bloom. Virginia liked the few weeks in the fall when the leaves held onto the trees. They clung to the branches not quite ready for winter to shake them off, but knowing the cold was inevitable. Winter never failed to arrive, and she disliked the cold more and more.

As she parked in front of the house, her phone buzzed in the cupholder. One missed call from her mother, who was probably sitting inside. "Hi, Mama."

There was no answer.

"Hello?" Virginia said again.

"Yes, who is this?" Her mother sounded startled.

"Mama, it's Virginia. Can't you see my car?"

"Why, yes! Why'd you call me if you're right outside?"

"Mama, I didn't . . ." Virginia let out a sigh and then laughed. It was better to laugh. "I'll be right in. I've got your milk."

"Virginia! Did you get the bread?"

"Yes, Mama, I've got the bread."

"Good. They're hungry."

Virginia's mother Betsy was seventy-three. Since leaving work she'd taken a liking to feeding the geese that flocked to her yard, and to needlepoint. She'd been an elementary school teacher for nearly thirty years and taught basic addition and subtraction to a room full of second graders. For most of her life, Virginia didn't understand how her mother could be so patient, but having a daughter of her own, Charlotte, had opened her eyes to a lot of things she hadn't seen before. Her father, Bill, was a cardiac surgeon and had been happily able to retire early, right around the time he became a grandfather to Charlotte. Being a grandfather seemed to slow him down, but his wife had also begun to slow, and he was ready to put the scalpel to rest. He was a help to Virginia, coming by the house to bring diapers or formula when Jimmy was on the road. He had also stayed the night a few times while she worked late at the hospital.

He'd gotten her that job too. Sure, she'd done well in nursing school, but her father was the reason that spot was secured.

Virginia couldn't come home as often as she wanted—Charlotte had started kindergarten, and Jimmy was working long hours. With each week that passed, she noticed her mother had forgotten something new: where she kept the salt, her renowned fudge pie recipe, the name of the dog.

When she knew Virginia was coming, her mother made sure to call and request a loaf of bread. She never forgot the bread. The geese had found a temporary home in the expanse of the Mays' backyard, pecking at the grass and leaving plenty of poop and feathers behind. Virginia wasn't sure if geese could feel happiness or love, but she was sure they enjoyed her mother's devotion. She treated them like the students she'd taught for so many years, talking to them as if they could respond with more than a honk or a squawk. She'd raised Virginia with the same kind of love and affection, but without another sibling, it was possible her mother loved her too much. She was a member of the PTA, had cheered as loudly as she could at every soccer game (and cried during Virginia's first and only goal), and had woken up at six o'clock every morning to ensure her lunch was packed. Virginia wasn't sure what she'd done to deserve any of this.

She walked into the house with the bread and the milk, but her mother was nowhere to be found. Her father sat on the sofa with his legs crossed and a cup of coffee in hand.

"She's already outside. I'm not sure a tornado could stop her from waiting." He sighed with relief at the sight of his daughter.

It had been several weeks since Virginia had been home. She kept in touch with phone calls and texts, but it had become easy for her to find excuses to avoid in-person visits. She was still learning how to care for her mother and didn't feel ready to stop being a daughter. Her father did his best to tell Virginia if it was a good day or a bad day before she visited, but he didn't need to tell her that by now—the good were outnumbered.

"I wish I could come see you and Charlotte more often, but I don't like to leave her much now," her father said.

"I know, Daddy."

Virginia had learned to expect her mother's worsening condition, but there was no timetable for her, or anyone, to follow. She wished there had been instructions. A list that said "And on day 264, expect your parent or significant other to hallucinate." But the not knowing had allowed her to be hopeful for the good days as well as the bad.

"Is Jimmy home tonight?" her father asked.

"He picked up Charlotte and took her out for ice cream. He leaves for a quarry in Mooresville on Monday. They're finally starting to pay him what he deserves."

"You just let me know if you need anything." Her father looked tired. Virginia was sure he'd been up late with her mother for the sounds of footsteps in the hallway or tapping on the window. There was no one there, her father knew that, but he checked for her every time.

Virginia put the milk in the fridge and walked out onto the porch. Her mother was running her hands along the weathered stones of the wall in the middle of the field. There was a pond on the other side of the wall, closer to the trees, where some of the geese slept in the night. She was sure the wall had once been much taller and longer, but over the years stones had fallen from it. Moss grew along the stones, weeds sprouting in the gaps. Virginia stepped off the porch, small blades of grass tickling her ankles. As she walked toward her mother, she noticed her hair was the same gray color as the wall, the white in it shimmering as the sun peered from behind the clouds. There was little blue left in the sky, and small drops of rain began to fall. The geese wouldn't come until the storm cleared.

"It's starting to rain," Virginia said. "You'd better come inside, Mama." Her mother seemed dazed, but not alarmed, as Virginia took her arm and they walked back to the house. She wore a distant expression on her face, a mix of wonder and fear, like she was lost, but wanted to be found. It was as if her mother had floated away, to somewhere else. Virginia remembered a few lines from a book she'd recently started to read. It sat on her nightstand collecting dust for longer than she wanted to admit. The book promised to be a guide, "a helping hand" to families in their journey with Alzheimer's. Virginia didn't like the word "journey." A journey, to her, implied a victorious ending, or a lesson learned, and she struggled to see the light at the end of this tunnel. Eventually, she put her cynicism aside, and as she started to read, she found solace in the writing. The book was full of hard truths, but it preached a certain amount of acceptance and letting go that she tried to appreciate. "You have to accept that they're not coming back to you, but that doesn't mean you can't go to them." Virginia wanted to be with her mother somewhere, wherever that was.

As they stepped inside, her mother said, "Virginia, I've just remembered I have a conference with Richie Bradshaw's parents. He's been such a pain in my behind lately. Of course, I'd never tell them that, but I just can't get him to keep his mouth shut!"

Her mother hadn't taught, let alone been back to the school, in years. Virginia guessed Richie Bradshaw was probably in his twenties by now. She glanced at her father. He shook his head. *Play along*, he mouthed.

Virginia took a deep breath.

"Mama, Daddy and I actually called the school this morning. We thought you could use a day off, and they've made sure to find a substitute. You've given that school enough of your time."

Her mother wore the same confused expression and let the weight of her body sink into the couch.

"Well, alright," she said with a huff. "Virginia, will you make me a cup of hot cocoa? I think we've got milk in the fridge."

Virginia warmed the milk in a pot on the stove and emptied a powdery packet of hot chocolate into a mug. Her mother loved hot cocoa, so Virginia had started buying her a new mug every year for Christmas. By now the cabinet was stuffed full of bright, multicolored ceramic. She chose the "I love you to the moon and back" mug, decorated with stars and a small cow sitting on the curve of a crescent moon. Her mother had said this to her often while tucking her into bed.

"I love you to the mooooon and back, my little love." Then her mother would kiss her forehead and leave the door open just a crack to let some light in. Virginia did this with Charlotte now, every night.

Virginia waited for the soy milk to cool slightly, blew the steam from the top, and took it to her mother.

"What's wrong with this milk?" her mother said with a hard swallow.

"That's just soy milk, Mama. Nothing wrong, just a little different."

"Tastes funny. That's fine I guess, as long as it's not spoiled."

Virginia smiled to herself. She'd expected this moment.

When her mother's short-term memory first began to dwindle, their family physician had reassured them that it was just old age. Then it was mild cognitive impairment, but the progression was slow, "nothing to be concerned about," he said. Virginia was twenty-two at the time, getting settled into a new home with Jimmy, and the thought of raising a child hadn't even come to her mind. She was getting ready to finish an undergraduate degree in biology at William Peace University and was looking into a career as a family nurse practitioner. Her father had wanted her to go out of state, but Virginia sensed that she needed to be close to home. Jimmy was the light of her life, but she wasn't staying in rural North Carolina for him alone. It was her mother, really, and her own fear and sadness, that kept her there.

Virginia had Fridays off her senior year, and she dropped in and brought her mother lunch at school when she could. One afternoon in January, Virginia came in with two sandwiches and a bowl of soup. Her mother's students were laughing, some of them with their little hands covering their mouths to hide the sound.

In a chorus of high-pitched voices, they called, "Hi, Miss Virginia!" Her mother had a strange look of embarrassment on her face, and her cheeks were spotted with a rosy flush.

"Miss Virginia, Mrs. May said she saw a funny man outside the window! She said he was wearing a yellow hat and flowery shorts!"

They giggled as Charlie McAlister pointed to the window at the back of the classroom. There was no one there.

"Well, that's silly! Hey guys, do you think you can be good while I talk to Mrs. May for a second? We'll be right outside."

She took her mother's arm.

In the hall, her mother said she was certain there was a man in a yellow hat and flowered shorts standing outside the classroom window.

"I can even tell you what kind of flowers they were! They were roses. I've never seen a man with roses on his shorts."

Her mother said she wasn't afraid of the man; she didn't wonder how he'd gotten there, or who he was. She seemed sort of bewildered, genuinely surprised, and curious. It was her childlike sort of wonder that scared Virginia. Suddenly, she felt very old. She knew there would come a day when she would have to care for her mother and her father too. Virginia suspected that every child knew that day would come. But she'd never imagined it would come so soon.

She and her father took her mother to the hospital shortly afterward, where she was formally diagnosed with Alzheimer's disease. Virginia felt angry that they hadn't gotten it right the first time, but the doctors insisted this, too, would be a slow progression. "At least another ten years," they said. They were fast approaching year eleven.

Her mother had other hallucinations, more and more bizarre. Once she saw a small man on the ceiling fan in their bedroom, and four years into her diagnosis she was convinced her husband had been having an affair. *"I saw the woman, Bill. She was wearing an emerald-green dress."* There wasn't much need to talk her out of it. Every hallucination was quick. It was like she'd been caught in a brief trance, and moments later she returned to reality, flipping through the channels or poking at her needlepoint.

The thunder began to rumble in the distance. There was a quiet pitter-patter on the roof that quickly grew to the sound of waves crashing in the ocean. Her father turned to his wife and said, "Sweetheart, the storm is close now." Instead of walking back to her bedroom like she usually did, her mother stood with her face very close to the glass door, watching as the rain poured and the branches thrashed together. But she wasn't interested in the storm. Her eyes were fixed on the middle of the field. She put her palm on the glass, condensation forming around the shape of her hand.

"Bill, do you see that little girl out there?"

"No, Betsy," he said. "But I'm sure you do."

He said it in a sort of endearing way, to the woman he loved and treasured more than anything, as though he knew she could see that little girl. She could see her clear as day.

"Bill, she looks so kind. She's got pretty green eyes and hair the shade of buttercups or sunshine rays. Bill, she looks just like . . . just like our . . ."

"Our Virginia," he said, and her mother said, "Yes. Yes, our Virginia."

Virginia's mother had forgotten her name. She lifted her head to see her father's sympathetic eyes. She wanted to think this was just a bad day, but she knew her mother would forget how to walk, how to eat. She would need constant attention like a newborn. Virginia had thought about this moment, expecting to be overwhelmed with sadness, but that wasn't quite what she felt. Perhaps it was because this woman did not resemble her mother anymore. She had been fading away. It was strange, Virginia thought, to not recognize her own mother.

After only a half hour, the clouds parted and the storm began to clear. Virginia went outside with her mother and the loaf of bread. Her father sat inside, looking through the glass door as Virginia placed an arm around her mother and guided her down the steps to the meadow. The geese had already begun to waddle toward them, making small squawks and honks. Their feathers were a mixture of white and gray and brown, with the lighter colors fading into the darker, like paints running together on a palette. The leaves of the trees and blades of grass glistened and twinkled with the leftover rain. The water seeped into Virginia's shoes. Her mother had left her fleece slippers on. They would probably be ruined, but that didn't seem to matter. The sunlight grazed her mother's shoulders and the profile of her face as she tore the soft bread into pieces and threw them to the geese. She looked angelic. The rays broke through the clouds with an almost holographic effect. Virginia wanted desperately to touch them, to hold the light in her hands, but as she opened her palm, they slipped through her fingers and onto the ground.

the   rays
slipped
through
her fingers

The Quietness of Litterfall

Veronica Nation

After "Birches" by Robert Frost

I have seen the chalk of aspens floating like dust
alongside enduring leaves that wilt as the fading poppies do.
The powder of the bark falls in slow motion to meet
the gray ground of newly deadened grass.

I like to think the eyes carved in white trunks
watch the rot of the earth become enveloped
by a heap of shedding golden foliage. Then,
as the frosted ground might melt into itself
like rain into a lake, the eyes of the aspens blink
just in time to miss the sprouts of yellow-green buds
unfolding on the thin limbs of ripened trees.

But spring is unreachable this time of year,
when life pauses and daylight shrinks.
When the stems of aspen leaves still clutch
the slippery white limbs extended out
like knights wielding swords made of splinters.

And so I wait. I wait and I watch
the tremble of leaves in a restless wind
bending and wrinkling in ever-dimming light.
I watch them fall kaleidoscopically
to a fate of decay at the base of their hosts,
their veins darkening as the sky does,
their smooth edges crisping.

Searching for Remnants

Veronica Nation

We used to try to float the common leaves of cottonwoods
and the needles of spruces and pines
in the stream of rainwater pooling against pavement.
So many stuck to the sides and we would be left
chasing the ones that made it through the pebbles.

Outside that dull yellow house, the one we fought in most,
we danced in the wind and rain as children do, unaffected
by the decay of autumn. When the leaves began to slough
and the pine cones became stale in shade and damp soil,
we would stomp until it all became mush under our shoes.

And through the houses
and all the change that autumn brings,
you always found a tree to climb.
And sometime before you stopped being a child
and I stopped dancing in the rain,
you fell from an unsteady limb

and the fall was not so gracious
as the leaves we used to watch autumn carry down.
And through the stitches and resetting of bone,
the trees begged for you to pick their dying leaves off,
to hasten the delivery of what pushes leaves to fall in the
      first place—
to stop the growth before the loss worsens.

And through the grieving of all I have left of you,
I forage for pictures in my mind of our small hands
pushing fallen leaves through currents of rain.
I search for the remnants
of cottonwoods floating in those streams,

and I chase them.

stop

the

growth

before

the loss

worsens

Dental Records

Isabel Glass

Most everyone I love was born in October. The colors are turning, as they always do, and I am reflecting. My brother says time moves quicker as you age because each second becomes a smaller portion of your life even though the length of your seconds remains the same. That might explain my growing pains, my urge to preserve all that is meant to go, a distrust of units by which we try to measure ourselves and each other. At night, I run my tongue over the grooves of my mouth to try to find answers. I am usually left wondering what hides in the ridges of my twenty-eight teeth.

Allison's mother was spring cleaning today, though it's autumn now, and clutter always seems to stay. As of this month, they are moving north and starting again. Allison sent me a photo of her baby teeth that were found within the mess. I wonder where mine are—my first two, blue after the accident, and the others falling out in city dumps and secretly in class. I often yearn for the time when plucking baby teeth from gums was the worst pain. I had to get four pulled once, for crowding. I didn't understand, then, that their removal was premature, that they had not had the proper time to disappear, that teeth are supposed to fall out small and delicate, that they fall out when their nerve roots are thoroughly decayed, their own way of regulating pain of having to let go. I was given four monstrous fangs that day, still numb with Novocain. I remember wishing to split those teeth open, right in two, and to watch what spilled out. I remember wishing for an explanation.

This October, I am trying to save a houseplant. It used to be Anna's, before she gifted it to me the night that we moved out—a final symbol of our shared lives. She had to remind me about the right levels of sunlight. Neither of us knew how much water was enough. Anna, tender and fierce, no longer resisting the tides of goodbyes. Me, heaving against the undertow. Now, Allison has a room full of plants across the country. She is good at being a mother, at keeping them loved and sunbathed. A while ago, I left Anna's plant in my car only to find it, hours later, shriveled and brown from the late summer sun. I thought maybe the plant had shriveled out of spite; overcome with sudden anger, a sadness she could not turn away from.

Recently, I've realized that her roots need more room to grow. They, like my teeth, are out of space. The plant is too big for the same pot she was born into years ago by now. Roots are too tangled. Dirt is too old—brittle and faded. While tending to her in the afternoon light, I think of all the Octobers I've lived. I think of all the Octobers those I love have lived. I find myself frozen in fear that unrooting this plant will be her end. I don't want that. I find myself wanting to hold water in my hands, to become it, to run downstream and then turn the bend and come home. These days, I close my eyes and see orange. I wish I could count the falling leaves, could predict who will leave me next.

Someone once told me about a species of trees that, when one dies in a grove, cries sap onto the soil to try to resurrect them. I searched for this yesterday, but nothing came up. I first wondered if I'd imagined it—a memory of something that hadn't been mine. Then I wondered if she had lied to me. I suppose I am glad that she did. I want to bathe in a world where resurrection is possible. I want to cry sap onto the soil of relationships that have become too tangled for a repotting and resurrect what could have been.

I wake up wanting to say thank you. My teeth often feel like they have shifted overnight. I live with the impression that they should have stopped moving as a teenager, when the braces came off and I learned of the fragility of past selves and when, in an October, I realized I needed to grow in new and strange directions. It's not a sharp pain anymore—in fact, it's dull, a pulse in the background, growing aches; a memory just around the corner. Forgiveness, tucked away in the blanket chest behind the door, surrounded by teeth and fallen leaves.

The Trouble with Tenderness

Gita Labrador

When I set the string of pillows in a pot by the window
I pray the plant will teach me something of patience.

Its leaves, plump as the pads on my fingers,
fall one by one over the next two weeks

until one day I find it a wilted snarl
of itself, clinging to life by fragile buds.

Its shoots are tiny, hopeful things
so I act on an impulse to save

without knowing how—thirty
reckless minutes of plunging fingers

in the dirt, snatching sprouts from lifeless
stems, windowsill gone black with rot

and wither—after all that, the remains lie
limp, worse off by my muddied hands.

So I carry the pot to the garden, hoping
the sun will save what I can't. Its leaves fall

like a sick person's hair—sometimes, I'm told,
it's to make room for new growth. How can I

possibly know the difference, blundering
through the days on the edge of survival?

This, I think, is my trouble with tenderness:
living and dying so often feel the same.

Cold beneath the Mountain Ash

Shaun Anthony McMichael

Lately, it feels like you and I are two different
seasons unable to abide the other for long
before moving to another part
of our little world. Our house
by the mountain ash starts getting cold

in mid-September. You hibernate under
goose-down drifts of duvets
while I sit under the ash tree, soaking
up the last inspirations of sun
while I add these pages to the falling leaves.

When I pull us up in the car and park beneath the tree,
I want to wait with you there, but you lunge out.
Shirking away from the cold air, you claim, not
running away from me. But I'm not so sure, the cold
and I being one and the same most of the time.

To be fair, I didn't know what I wanted until now,
so I've never told you. *Breathe in the air of me, of us,
with me. Take in this air, this time beneath the mountain ash
and see how its crushed orange berries are its tears
and let this seeing together be a salve, if not salvation.*

We can bear each other the longest as shoulder seasons
of sorts, when we are shoulder to shoulder, ensconced
in down and sleep. And even then, whimsy wakes me.
And then it's you who will murmur for me to wait
with you there for a while where it's warm

but I lunge free. I go to greet the cold that waits
beneath the mountain ash where I can watch the falling
leaves and add a page to their number. I've never asked
what you want. Yet I realize now that it's something
that could keep us warm for longer than this.

add

these

pages

to the

falling

leaves

Stop-Motion

Kim Weldin

Sam sat with her back flat against one side of the city bus, squished in a row of strangers, all stuffed and sticking to one another in fat winter coats like marshmallows in a plastic bag. Sam looked especially swollen in her oversized black puffer coat with the faux fur-lined hood. She was riding the bus home from work, sitting among a succession of unfamiliar faces.

She swiped the cracked screen of her phone in an upward motion with a black fingerless glove, scrolling past unwanted ads for meal subscriptions and workout apps. She didn't look up except for when a woman with rosy red cheeks and frazzled gray hair asked if the seat next to her was taken. Before Sam could respond, the woman plopped down in the seat with bulging plastic bags of groceries and heavy sighs. A cold jar of pasta sauce pushed through the bottom of one of the bags and knocked hard against Sam's exposed ankle bone. Sam pulled her foot in closer to her body.

Sam ignored the woman, remained in her own world, and kept scrolling for square images that spoke to her—city skylines carving the sky with sharp, steel architecture; light sandy beaches contrasting against surreal blue skies; charming row houses in rainbow pastels lining cobblestone roads. It was a way she passed the time in transit—seeking out pictures of places she'd like to travel, places she'd like to see with her own eyes. She almost missed her stop scrolling through a sea of digital images of Santorini, the lurid blue of the Aegean Sea on the screen making her pupils dilate wide with excitement.

Sam got off the bus and started walking home, then stopped at the QFC to pick up something for dinner. She traveled through the grocery store where signs hung overhead designating the aisles: SOUPS, PASTA, INTERNATIONAL. In the checkout line, copies of *Travel + Leisure* loomed from behind the black bars of a magazine rack, a bold graphic font teasing the "Top Ten Travel Destinations of 2022."

When she got home, she sat on her upcycled sofa and stewed, trying to remember the last time she'd taken a trip. She was overdue for one, that was for sure, but her job at the video store didn't afford her the luxury of travel. And although she obsessively scoured and saved travel pictures from Instagram to her phone, she wasn't eager to spend her own money going anywhere at the moment. It didn't feel safe or responsible to travel. She'd rather save her money.

Five years ago, Sam had taken a ferry from Seattle to Whidbey Island, where the landscape was so picturesque—like an illustration from a Little Golden Book come to life. She'd loitered in a field of soft grass, sitting on her knees and trying to touch the wild rabbits humming and nibbling near her until an older local fussed at her.

"Don't touch the rabbits. They carry diseases," the woman warned Sam, as she'd naively stretched a long arm toward the rabbits.

She'd observed tall painted totem poles with faded paints in primary colors towering above her at Lone Lake and picked up smooth rocks that looked like glass underwater. The shiny rocks turned dull in her palm when she took them out of the water and exposed them to the air.

That was the last trip she'd taken—a trip that taught her some things look better from far away, some things look better in pictures than they actually appear. Soon she'd discover this applied to people, too.

Sam arrived early each morning to manage the Magnolia Movie store in the University District. She rode the bus or her bike to work, traveling the hilly streets of Seattle, from

---

the colorful sculptures and murals that lined Fiftieth Street in Fremont to the maple leaf lined sidewalks of Ravenna. She went over and under bridges and freeways, passing tent cities of the houseless blooming rapidly in all colors of the rainbow.

A man stood guard outside the entrance to the video store like a sentinel with a tent bag slung over one shoulder.

"Mornin'," he said, shooting Sam a friendly, toothless grin.

Sam kept her eyes on her keys as she fumbled to fit them into the door. When the key finally clicked and the lock sighed open, she smiled amiably at the man, nodding hello, and made her way into the store, pulling the heavy glass and metal doors shut behind her.

At work, Sam stocked videos slowly and methodically. She organized the videos by genre, collection, director. She studied the summaries on the backs of the cases, absorbing the names of film critics and publications. She was familiar with various movie magazines—*Fangoria, Filmmaker*. She knew the classics and contemporary films in the Criterion Collection, and she could list the filmography of John Waters from *Pink Flamingos* to *A Dirty Shame*.

When she first saw Ben, she'd watched him idling in front of the Staff Favorites shelf for almost half an hour. She stood behind the rental counter casually checking him out while checking out customers. In typical Seattle style, he wore a rust-orange beanie and jean jacket. Sam thought he looked like a hipster from an indie rock band or a homeless person, but she couldn't size him up from far away. She watched him stare at the movies, struggling to select one. Occasionally he'd lift one hand languidly from his jacket pocket and pick up a video to examine it. She observed him as he turned the DVD case in his hand, noticing the dirt under his nails, and then her eyes traveled up to the bristly blond hairs on his face. She suddenly felt self-conscious—he might be reading one of her staff reviews on the Post-it notes that were stuck to the cases.

Finally, he wandered over to the counter holding a DVD from the Staff Favorites shelf.

"Who's Sam?" he asked.

His blue eyes were red rimmed, and his sandy, shaggy hair stuck out of the sides of his orange beanie.

"That's me," Sam said, self-consciously pushing her oversized black frames up her thin nose, back to where they were supposed to sit.

She wondered if he was disappointed that Sam, the staff member who'd recommended the violent thriller *Blue Ruin*, was a woman.

"You have good taste," he said.

"Thanks," she said. "This one is really good."

"Cool. I'm Ben, by the way," he said.

"Enjoy the movie," Sam said, smiling awkwardly and waiting for him to say something else.

"Have a good night," Ben said, stepping out into the black Seattle sky and out of her line of sight, like a movie transition fading from one scene to the next.

It was fall in Seattle, and the sky turned as black as charcoal every day around four in the afternoon. Something about the day turning dark so early made people get squirrely, and Sam sensed something strange brewing in the air around her.

After work Sam walked into her dark Craftsman duplex and turned on an old floor lamp she'd found discarded on the side of the road. The light flickered and buzzed—it was probably a fire hazard. There was nothing good to eat in the house, but the thought of going out and spending money was unappealing, so she heated up a dented can of soup and sat down on the sofa with her phone, pulling her feet up under her and resting the warm bowl on her lap.

She swiped through pictures on her phone screen, stopping on a silhouette of a woman walking on a rocky beach, waves crashing majestically against massive black rocks that jutted out of the edge of the water and scattered across the sand like sharks' teeth. The caption read: "Thousands of people seek travel experiences that transform them, experiencing life-changing travel . . ."

Sam clicked the link to a website on transformational travel: a new type of travel, popular among millennials, in which travelers sought experiences that made them see the world through new eyes. It was a step up from traveling somewhere to gain world experience and experience different cultures—travel that transformed you permanently.

"Bullshit," Sam said through a mouthful of vegetable soup. The words echoed in the empty house. Her spoon clinked against the edge of the empty soup bowl.

The concept of transformational travel seemed pretentious and imprudent. Sam shrewdly saved her money, scared to spend it on anything too frivolous. Her clothing was all thrifted and in monotone black, a dependable uniform that made it easy to recycle outfits between washes where no one would notice.

She was devoted to sustainability and hyperaware of her own carbon footprint, always reheating leftovers and reusing tea bags, laying the bags out to dry on the kitchen counter until they were ready for a second use. She saved the extra packets of crackers that came with her takeout orders—*just in case*—and rinsed out empty pasta sauce and jam jars, repurposing them as water or wine glasses.

Besides, she could drink wine from Spain or France in the

comfort of her own home while watching *The Spirit of the Bee-hive* or *Breathless*. That was transformative enough for her. She could easily lose herself when watching a film—zoning out, disappearing into the set of the movie, like a film dissolving from one scene to the next. She'd disassociate frequently—losing awareness of her surroundings, transporting into the life of a fictional character on the screen in front of her.

Sometimes Sam felt as though she were watching a movie of her own life—a voice invariably narrating her actions in her head. Other times she saw herself as the female lead in films as she watched them—in their profiles, the arc of a nose, the curve of a chin, the brown outline of hair around a pale, fragile face, like Eva in the black-and-white frames of *Stranger Than Paradise*.

The man was there almost every day now, standing in front of the video store, scaring customers away with his duffle bags and cardboard signs—his existence. He stood in front of the glass windows singing "Ramblin' Man," his voice bellowing, as loud as the screeching brakes of a garbage truck. Sam watched him through the windows as he harangued people walking on the sidewalks in front of the store.

Maybe I do need a transformational travel experience.

I'm twenty-eight and managing a video store, she thought.

Less and less people came into the store to rent movies, opting to stay safe at home with their streaming services: Netflix, Hulu, Amazon Prime, HBO Max. Streaming services were the enemy of the video store that supported her Seattle lifestyle, but the reality was she supported at least two of the services herself. Some of the only people who still frequented the store were lonely men who came to rent smutty adult films or stoned college kids who came to rent obscure cult

---

classics like *Troll 2*.

She rode the bus to work one day, riding under the Aurora Bridge past the famous Fremont Troll, looking out of the window at the tourists climbing on the sculpture to take pictures. The sculpture was a constant in her life, stuck in time and concrete, but she liked it that way. It was predictable, something she could count on.

Ben came in that day, clinging the bells on the glass door behind him, walking toward Sam with a hopeful look in his eyes.

"Got any more recommendations?" he asked, stuffing his hands into his jeans and smiling.

He kept coming in every few days after that, wearing the same outfit—a denim tuxedo and an orange beanie. He'd follow her around the store while she restocked the shelves, asking her opinions on documentaries and directors' techniques. She was only slightly surprised when he showed up one day and asked her out to dinner.

They went to a busy Thai restaurant in the University District, where they were seated at a tiny wooden table in the back of the restaurant next to the bathroom. People kept coming in and out of the bathroom, bringing pissy, soapy odors out with them.

Sam tried to concentrate on the green curry in the leaf-shaped pottery bowl in front of her. At the end of the meal, Ben's face froze with panic as he reached for his wallet.

"Shit," he said.

"Is everything okay?" she asked.

Sam thought maybe the spicy curry had traveled too quickly through his body—but Ben had only forgotten his wallet. When she placed her debit card on the table, he quickly corrected her.

"Actually, it's cash only," he said, shrugging his shoulders as if to say he was sorry.

Outside the restaurant a group of punk teens and a skinny pit bull were huddled around a bus stop. A girl with green hair and a torn black Suicidal Tendencies T-shirt blew cigarette smoke in their direction while a heavyset boy with short dreads and a spiked collar nodded to Ben as if he recognized him.

Sam locked eyes with the dog. They shared a look that said, *It's not my fault I'm here—in this particular place.*

They were sitting in the corner window of a Fremont cafe sipping Americanos from souvenir mugs that said WYOMING and FLORIDA and eating pastries on small, mismatched china.

"I want to get to know you more," Ben said, smiling.

A tiny flaky square of scone stuck to his bottom lip. Sam noticed a brown stain on one of his front teeth. Sam had been wondering if the stain was from smoking but never felt like asking him. She pondered on the point that she'd paid for the pastries and coffee.

"What do you want to know?" she asked, shrugging her shoulders up to her ears.

"Why do you work at the video store?" he asked.

"Did you know that there are less than two thousand video stores left in the whole country?" Sam asked.

"Yeah," he scoffed. "But do you think you'll work there forever?

"I don't know. I love movies. I guess the store reminds me of growing up and going to the video store with my family. It was an event. Something to look forward to on Friday nights. Everyone stays home and streams now."

"I get that," he said. "My mom was a librarian. Kind of similar."

She looked out the cafe window and tried to think of the similarities between video stores and libraries.

"I guess."

Ben was quiet. She wondered if he was bored or if he expected her to continue sharing more about herself—more things she didn't have the answers to yet.

She felt like she was always going through the motions in life, an endless series of motions that never meant anything, never made anything happen. She didn't like being interrogated by anyone about her personal life because they might find out that she didn't have anything under the surface worth seeing.

"So," he continued, after an uncomfortable thirty seconds of silence. "What else do you want to do? With your *life?*"

"Wow. Big question," she said. "I guess I haven't really thought about doing anything else. The store keeps me busy. I haven't told anyone this yet, but the store is probably going to close. No one really rents movies anymore. The owners haven't kept up with things. They're behind on rent. I think they're going to sell it."

"Sell what?" he asked.

"The store."

"That sucks. I guess you'll have to do something else then?"

"Actually, I've been saving up."

"For what?"

"The store. I want to buy it."

"Wow. How much have you saved?"

"Not much. Around ten thousand."

Sam immediately regretted disclosing this. She hadn't told anyone about her plan. Her cheeks were beginning to burn. She still didn't know Ben. She didn't know what he did for work or where he lived, but at the same time she didn't really care to know either. She'd been seeing him for over a month and wasn't sure why. She supposed his company was nice.

"Your turn," she said. "Are you ever going to show me where you live?"

Above the bed hanging in the center of the wall was a framed print, a landscape painting with three staggered sailboats, all of them sailing toward a lighthouse in the middle of the ocean. Sam felt Ben's warm breath, his mouth wet and moving, licking slowly at the space between her legs. She stared up at the picture. The water was a dark, deep bluish gray, almost black toward the bottom, and the sails were bright white, as white as the sheets on the bed that she was gripping. *Were these organic cotton?* Rough, scratchy brushstrokes blended the sky above in a combination of whites, yellows, and browns.

"I like this picture," she said.

"Huh?" Ben said, lifting his head up from between her legs.

He looked at her face turned toward the wall and saw Sam staring blankly at the painting.

"Oh yeah, that," he said. "Do you want me to stop?"

"No. It feels good," she said. "Keep going."

After she came, Ben went in the bathroom to wash his wet beard and brush his teeth. She sat up on the bed and looked around the room. She ran her hand across a white quilted coverlet. It felt soft, high-quality, like a high-end hotel matelassé.

When they left the house, Ben didn't lock the front door behind him.

"You don't lock your door?" Sam asked, pointing her elbows out suggestively toward the hidden edges of the neighborhood that transitioned into the public areas of the city.

"Nah, it's fine," he said, smirking and squishing his eyebrows inward.

She wondered why her question appeared to amuse him, as if he thought he was smarter than her. She thought about the sailboat print. It looked like something you'd find in the back of a T.J. Maxx.

"Are you seeing someone else?" she asked.

"Why would you ask me that?"

"I mean—is this really *your* house?"

She took her hands out of her jacket and crossed them over her chest, like she was trying to hold herself together. She felt like she'd exposed too much of herself to him within the last hour and she wanted to pull herself back together, as if her coat were a sleeping bag she could zip herself up and hide inside of.

He looked past her, looking over her shoulders at the houses on the other side of the street.

"Do you think I'm lying? Why would I lie about living here?" he asked, through a slightly clenched jaw.

"It's just—I noticed there were a lot of nice things—expensive things. Things a woman might have," she said.

"You think I can't have nice things because I'm a guy?" he scoffed.

She stood there waiting for an answer, trying to meet his eyes.

"You didn't have any pictures."

"Whatever," he said, waving a hand down as if he were shooing her off and started walking away.

She didn't follow him. She watched his back as he walked away, down the sidewalk and disappeared after he turned right at the corner of the street.

Sam came out of the store and pulled the doors toward her to lock them closed for the night. The thin, crunching sound of someone stepping on leaves startled her, and she gasped.

"Oh my God. You scared me," she said, holding her hand to her chest as she caught her breath.

She didn't recognize him at first, but it was Ben. They hadn't spoken in weeks.

"Sorry," he said. His pupils were tiny—the size of pencil tips, quivering in their centers.

"Are you okay?" she asked, searching his face.

"Yeah. Sorry I haven't called."

"It's okay," she said. "I'm heading home. Do you want to come over?"

Back at her place, Sam cooked brown rice and heated a can of black beans, layering the ingredients in glazed ceramic bowls. She took an old jar of salsa out of the fridge, sniffing it to make sure it was still edible, and then doled out cold spoonfuls on top of the warm rice. She sprinkled diced avocado on top and then handed him a warm bowl, noticing for the first time it had a chip on the edge.

He looked thinner than the last time she saw him. He ate a few forkfuls of rice and beans, and then put his bowl down on the coffee table, as if he wasn't hungry. He cleared his throat.

"I need to ask you something," he said, looking down at his legs on the sofa and scratching under his chin. The sound of his fingers on his beard made a bristly sound.

"Okay."

"I need a favor," he said. "I need to borrow some money."

Sam was silent. She didn't know what she'd expected. An apology? Answers?

"What?"

"Just two thousand—twenty-five hundred, if you can spare it."

She didn't know what to say. Words swam around in her head like fish inside a glass bowl. She was waiting for the words to come up to the surface, but her mouth wouldn't seem to open. Ben looked down at his boots and rubbed a wet leaf from the sole onto the floor. She stared at the leaf on the hardwood floor.

Sam's eyes continued glazing over as she stared at the floor. She could hear Ben talking, his words were moving around in her head, but she couldn't seem to move or speak.

He made a motion with his hands in front of her face trying to get her attention.

"Okay," she said.

"I'm in a bad place right now. I don't know who else to ask. I'll pay you back," he said, his hands jittering in his lap.

As Ben continued explaining his situation to her, her eyes traveled back to the wet leaf on the floor. She could tell that the leaf had been stuck to the edge of his boot for a while. It was dull and limp, its colors changed from a bright rust orange to a muddy blackish brown. She wondered when the leaf clung to the boot, becoming stuck there, wedged in between the thick rubber tread. The edges of the leaf weren't sharp and pointed, but dull and torn from traveling across the city sidewalks as he trampled through the neighborhood from the store to her house.

Sam was standing in security when her phone rang. She saw the name on the screen, pushed the red circle, and tossed her phone in the gray plastic tray. She imagined Ben back at the video store, looking through the locked glass doors, looking for her. She took off her boots and dumped them and her purse into another big plastic tray. She slid the trays across the table and walked through the metal detector.

On the other side of the line, she watched the trays as they traveled along the conveyor belt, pushing through the thick black belts that dangled down like long rubber eyelashes. She stood there, waiting to recognize the things that belonged to her—her black crossbody purse, her black boots. She collected them and traveled toward her gate.

She boarded the plane, moving slowly down the narrow aisles in search of her seat. It was a window seat near the back. She'd paid extra for it. She slid the plastic shade up and looked out of the window, oblivious to the woman across from her who shield her eyes in silent protest as the sun blinded her. She watched below as the blue water and square green tiles of land got smaller and smaller until all she could see were white clouds.

dull and

        torn

from traveling

across the city

sidewalks

City of Hope

Aiden Heung

Something has to give.
I hide in a brick apartment, joined by the wind
that sneaks in like a wrong idea.
                              Outside,
the sun settles, then scuffs to battered clouds,
forgotten as I'm forgotten,
though it's always here, far to touch, close to life,
minacious like police.

This is Shanghai—

and I know I'll leave like I have left all beautiful
and tragic things behind.

A lie.

I have nothing behind me
but memories misplaced like rusty keys,
and nothing before,
though I've been promised things:
sex, money, poetry,
a future
that glitters like a knife that can open any door.

I'm too old to disembark into life again,
a body cast into another,
a chafed dream
that ends like the day always ends,
with the sun bleeding to the last drop,

and the TV's talking hope.

Sixi Field

Aiden Heung

We choose a road hoed
out on the field carpeted
by rice stubs, whose

starched yellow grabs
earth, like firm resistance
to season's end. The drab

brightness dumps deeper
shade under weary trees
and pulls sky higher,

much higher than sun's
empyrean course.
Further out, the done

separation of sky and hills.
Low-flying sparrows, now
forced up, now driven

down, hungry for something.
We slow our steps, feed
on this scenery, consider

ourselves lucky, city
boys lost in uncitied land,
like an idea finding

a better translation—a necessary
conviction that we
can be useless and free,

like maple leaves redden
and fall to wind, the color
of fire and harvest.

firm resistance
to season's end

Meet Me under the Birches

Beck Anson

in their golden hour
when the geese fly south
overhead, when dense fog
settles on the river, obscuring
the mountains beyond.
Such a common thing,
a miracle nevertheless.
How? As you are, fallen
leaves and all. Meet me under
the birches in their golden
hour, where you've come
to find a long-lost friend,
the one you always were
but had forgotten about,
all mixed up in the chaotic
mess of living this human life.
Meet me under the birches
in their golden hour,
their leaves a bright light
against a stormy sky
and we are just goldenrod
and purple aster blowing
in a breeze. One by one,
we fell over. Under
the birches, we'll rise
as one.

Rebuilding

Beck Anson

And you?
When will you begin
that long journey into yourself?

The Rumi quote made sense at the time.
It said I needed to stop comparing myself to others
if I wanted to ever love myself again.

Said I needed to stop caring about what others
might think about me, about my body's appearance,
about my own trans experience.

Most of the time I just want to live my gender,
and let my gender live me. I want to see things
like bodies without trauma whispering in my ear.

I still shake, still sob, still lie down in the cold grass
behind the elementary school on clear November nights
asking for some kind of direction through all this change.

My shape is constantly evolving from curve to square, but really
I'm just the same kid who wants to fit inside a circle of peers,
who learned that the ground is hard but not unforgiving.

Who is still learning to let go of all that contains him
and that there are no rules—

just the ones he leaves behind

as he rebuilds himself again and again.

8

Beck Anson

Those autumn afternoons
on the dirt roads of Vermont

I drove through my grief
past the jerseys and silos

casting shadows on pastures
still viridescent, our life together

receding in the rearview mirror.
Over a year apart and here I am

holding onto our love like
the bittersweet oak leaves

in early November after the first
dusting of snow, their petioles clinging.

Twisting and turning my way through
the tears at the thought of all the years

of *goodnights* and *I love yous*. Steering
left then right in figure eights

with no particular destination,
no point B from point A.

Just the knowing of having left,
just the knowing of having loved.

If This Is How It Has to End

Marisa P. Clark

The sky's gray glower
crowds the picture window.
In the distance, dying leaves
in fiery colors warm the view.
A hawk alights on the arbor—
a Cooper's hawk, decked out
to match the day: topcoat
of black and charcoal feathers,
creamy breast flecked with flame.
Below, the vine's bare tendrils
twist and knot. The hawk tips
his head in studious hunt,
then drops into the clump
of grape leaves clinging
near the stump,
their green not fully spent.
His clumsy, juddering hops
rouse a small bird up
from hiding. It escapes
to who knows where.
The hawk flaps up to perch,
shakes out his feathers,
resumes his stately bearing.
He makes no secret
of himself, no apology
for appetite and desire
that come naturally
to his kind. I smile. I see
myself in him and you
in him, us two in the bird
that flew. If this is how
we have to end, at least we tried.

Ride to Work

Marisa P. Clark

I rarely take this route to work these days—
but when I reach Princeton Drive,
my head turns, automatic, up the block

toward the house you used to live in. Humble
tan adobe. Flat roof. Big tree littering the dirt yard
with leaves. A step up to the little porch

and the door opening into the living room:
TV, papasan big enough for two, and the bright blue
leather couch over which hung *Sky above Clouds*,

the Georgia O'Keeffe print I bought and framed,
a gift for you. We'd wake and walk to campus—
and that year on my birthday, the cottonwoods

dropped all their leaves to clatter on the street,
loud as good rain. The golden spades
crunched beneath our feet, and we held

hands. Later there'd be sex, good sex, long into the night—
and JLo or Madonna or Marc Anthony on repeat
to match our tempo, disguise your cries—there

in your bedroom, a converted garage
two steps down from the kitchen where we'd
finished off a home-cooked meal and four-berry pie

with your French roommates here on foreign exchange
and debated the virtues of Nutella and the different
words we had for the same things. *Banana*—

that's what they called the median strip
with the turn lane to your house. I called you
girlfriend, lover, love—you introduced me to your parents

as your "ride to work." That spring I went alone
into the playhouse in your backyard. Shed-sized box
of weathered wood. A door I had to duck to enter.

A window streaked with long-dried rain
through yellow dust. I inked our initials in a heart
on the ceiling. I carved those letters deep. They must be

long gone. Sanded off. Painted over. Or the whole
structure taken down and used for scrap. Whatever
their fate, they outlasted us. You moved away, and I

moved on. Like now. I press the gas, don't take
the turn. No reason to ride past.

leaves
clatter
on the
street,
loud as
goodrain

Same Old,
Same Old

Marisa P. Clark

New morning, same table and chair
of rough-hewn ponderosa pine. Same
glaring sky framed in the picture window.
A stillness, as if nothing happens, nothing
changes. So what changes? The weather,
of course. The seasons. The birds who alight
in the trees. The trees. The vitex tree
that in summer is lushly leafed with spears
of lavender blooms that sing with bumblebees
and hummingbirds
                              is brown now, leaves crisp
and branches exposed, flowers gone to seed
the nuthatches, warblers, and bushtits eat.
Those whose faith depends on sameness
are doomed to disillusionment. What fool
fears change? I was that fool. How I cried
the day a windstorm felled the piñon
that stood strong for years and grew,
shaded the yard, sheltered birds,
and was my constant view. How I cried
when I lost you. At first, I tried
a lilac bush, no luck. Now
I have the vitex, twice my height
and roundly squat. I plant
myself in this same chair at this same table
I once shared with you, and stare awhile
out the window I replaced last year,
then get up—
                    face what today has in store.

The Definition of Home

Taylor Stanton

She tells me over a piece of cinnamon pie. Its creamy consistency reminds me of crème brûlée. The rich brown slice stands out against the white tulip table.

"Doesn't everyone plan to move at a certain age?" I ask.

"I might have to move sooner than expected," she says, glancing at her lap.

Nothing clicks. I am often oblivious with my mother, caught in my own world and the dynamic we used to have. I take another bite of pie.

"The layer between the siding and the house is rotted. The siding was cracked. I wanted your grandpa to fix it before water got in there, but it's already rotted."

My grandpa spent the day before drilling holes in the siding. He drilled one hole and found nothing beneath. No rim joists. He drilled four holes to prove that the joists truly had rotted away, though one would have sufficed. Rim joists hold the bones of a home together. When they're gone, there's nothing left to keep the world from leaning. It's expensive to keep life upright.

Yellow leaves pelt the sliding glass door as my thoughts rush in and out, mimicking the November wind outside. I walk through the possibilities left by yesterday's conversation. Clink. Clink. Clink. The leaves sound like glasses touching after a toast. I want to blame them for distracting me from writing, but my mind is already gone. I'm no longer at my desk.

I'm turning past a bronze mailbox nailed to a post that's not quite tall enough to meet a car window. I hear the familiar crunch of gravel under my tires. I pass the cluster of pines where we buried our beloved Labrador retriever. If I got out of the car, I'd tread through waist-high grass and find river rocks stacked in a pile. I drive over the culvert past the monstrous wild blackberry bush that only produced watery fruit one summer and the place where purple milkweed always blooms. There's the small stream I followed one winter. Trudging along the snow-covered ground, I discovered a perfect frozen circle. One step on the ice and my entire body was immersed in frigid water. I can still feel the way my breath caught. When I turn the corner of the drive, a familiar house appears framed by several trees. This view always makes me smile.

The wind throws leaves at my door again and again, each rap on the glass a stern reminder. All things have a life. Change comes repeatedly regardless of the season. It feels like it happens overnight, but change doesn't have idle hands. Every autumn, you wait for trees to burst into new colors. Each time you look for change, the leaves are green. One day, you walk outside and everything is suddenly different. If all things have a life, then all things have an end.

The next morning, I get a text at 6 a.m.: "Should I put the porch urns in the barn for the guys to take?"

Today, men will look through the discarded objects of our lives. The red tin barn housed things that were unused or unclaimed. Left-behind relics of a marriage and a childhood. My father and I would jump on the old trampoline sitting halfway under the barn's awning. We ruined many pairs of white socks. He sang "Born to Be Wild," ball cap backward on his head while bouncing me higher. The trampoline was my getaway spot after he was gone. I would lie on my back taking in the expanse of sky within full view of the kitchen window. My mother never touched the trampoline except to drag it up to the place it sits now.

A basketball goal lives in the barn too, collecting cobwebs and dust. It sat at the concrete in front of the garage during my elementary years. I had tried my father's favorite sport. I broke three pairs of glasses and scored many embarrassment points. I fixed the idea that we'd ever connect over athletics. We practiced dribbling and shooting some evenings. The thud of the ball and the ringing that follows still echo in my mind. He said shooting a basket was like reaching your hand into a cookie jar. I watched my mother tow the goal up the barn's steep hill by herself several years later. In that moment, she was the strongest person I knew. Her determination made her seem fearless.

Dusty, long-forgotten boxes remain among the unwanted. A rusted workout bench and push mower have pined in the barn for over a decade, never collected by their owner. They are homes for spiders and packed-away memories.

Should she keep the urn planters? What else will she throw away? My mother doesn't have a lot of options. Being forced to sell the house she designed is devastating and embarrassing but utterly liberating. She works through her to-do list at a pace that can only result in a breakdown. She doesn't sleep at night. Clearing out the barn is a final cleanse, an official closing of a life that ended long ago.

Though she planned to sleep in this house for decades more, the burden of being the sole caretaker has been a weighty one. Her shoulders slumped every time there was a repair. The weight bore down on her through my younger years. She'd never say it, but we were living above our means those days. Slowly, somehow, the ability to stay afloat in her beach house in the woods simply receded like the tide. My mother just wanted someone to take care of her. She wanted to be a girl again.

Life gets away from you.

Someone comes to clean the gutters. My grandpa bush

hogs the brush. Someone fixes the upstairs heat. My child-hood easel goes to two young, brilliant creatives. I once used it to paint portraits of my tropical Walmart fish. My mother carries a green paisley armchair to the barn. Someone power-washes the siding so it glows like a smile in a toothpaste commercial. Someone stains the deck golden where we used to drink lemonade and sunbathe. My red Flyer wagon and tricycle are wheeled to the barn. My grandpa replaces box-turtle-bitten and snow-pulled-down porch screens. My bulletin board is measured and delivered to a family friend. My mother puts the iron urns out for the junk collectors.

I thought this house would be a place I could always land, a place to come home for the holidays, bring the children I may or may not have, share stories and relive our glory days. Home is more than a space, I know, but this goodbye will be hard.

Goodbye to the walls that sheltered me through every age. The hoard of Beanie Babies. The tiny china tea set. The middle school diary I hid in the closet. The prom dresses and the copy of *Fifty Shades of Grey* I snuck under the wicker shelf lined with sweaters. The mark I left in the granite countertop. The way we whispered to each other from upstairs to downstairs on quiet nights. The idea of what life was going to be before I knew who I was going to be.

Goodbye to the oak trees that are my oldest companions. When their leaves rustle in the wind, they sound like waves coming to shore. Close your eyes and let the breeze tousle your forever fuzzy baby hairs. These trees dropped twigs for me to poke the mud and stir watery grass cocktails of my own creation. I once pressed the dainty flowers that grow at their base.

Goodbye to the grass I frolicked in and the child I used to be. The wild I used to be. There will be no more dancing during woodsy walks. I come home to a different house now and no longer see only branches stretching across open sky. I no longer have a tree to call my own. If life doesn't work out, there's no falling back to old places and patterns. There will be no bedroom with forgotten trinkets lining the dresser and old clothes in the closet. This is the last mark of childhood before it is over. I was holding out hope that a piece of the past would never end. Children desperately want to grow up. I would love to go back and reclaim my freest self.

I don't want to lose this place that is my mother's and still part mine.

But life cuts through plans. I don't know who will make their home in what was once ours. I don't recognize the door my mother will unlock in the future. I don't know where she'll park her car or what she'll see from her window.

Evening shadows snuggle into me as I listen to my mother's voice on the phone. We find reasons for her to look forward to moving, taking comfort in closer movie theaters and clean slates. Memories tumble out of our mouths, and our conversation becomes a eulogy. We praise those early years and the walls that held them. I can hear her lips twitch upward. We belly laugh at our good life. And my greatest wish is that we will always be like this: the two of us on the phone for hours laughing in the dark, no matter where we are.

October Morning Raking Leaves

Joan Mazza

On a tarp I carry oak and tulip poplar leaves
into the woods, spend half a day moving them
from here to there as if I'm doing work

while the wind blows them back across the yard.
I'm little more than a leaf here—temporary,
drying into lines and fragile webs.

From the window, leaves are small animals
running in a herd from west to east. They stop
in unison, a flock of grackles before moving on.

Shovel snow and the wind blows it back
over the stairs, makes dunes like desert sand.
I let it be and wait until weather and nature

have their way with me. Where else should
I wait until I can't stand up alone?
The new roof will hold long after I am dust.

Here Comes Another Winter

Joan Mazza

Ahead of the cold front, gusts pick up
and brittle leaves come down. Temps
drop under a mottled sky patched
with blue, white, clouds of gray.
From my perch on the back porch

I watch leaves drift down, twirling
on air currents to land face down
on the deck and ground—yellow beech
and tulip poplar, blotchy brown
of red and white oak around my feet.

These bands of leafy showers rain down
between quiet pauses. No bird chirps.
Acorns fall and knock on wooden steps.

My eleventh winter here approaches,
yet this landscape still surprises—trees
let go of all they've made, dump their tons
of foliage that drift light as feathers,
to return to earth. I don't cut down the nearly

dead willow because it's a perch, resting
place for birds above the pond. In snowstorms,
the old tree bows down over the frozen pond—
lacy bridge of ice before it stands again.
It bends and doesn't crack.

Contributors

Susan Alexander is a Canadian poet and writer living in British Columbia on Nexwlélexm/Bowen Island, the traditional and unceded territory of the Squamish people. Susan's work has appeared in anthologies and literary magazines throughout Canada, the US, and the UK. She is the author of two collections of poems, *Nothing You Can Carry* (2020) and *The Dance Floor Tilts* (2017) from Thistledown Press. Her suite of poems called *Vigil* won the 2019 Mitchell Prize for Faith and Poetry, while some of her other work has received the Vancouver Writers Fest and Short Grain awards.

Mona Anderson is a retired mental health therapist living in the New Hampshire countryside with her husband, cats, and various other sentient beings. She is coauthor of *The Art of Building a House of Stone.* Her work has appeared in *Penning the Pandemic: An Anthology of Creative Writing from the Beginning of the COVID Era, Post Script: An Anthology of Postcard Poetry*, and *Pleasures Taken*, a Writing It Real anthology. Other poems will be published in the fall 2022 issue of *Constellations: A Journal of Poetry and Fiction* and in the spring 2023 issue of *Soul-Lit*, a journal of spiritual poetry.

Beck Anson (he/they) is a mad frolicker and dandelion picker. His work appears in *Rattle, RHINO, Humana Obscura*, and others. Their poem "I Admit Myself to the Psych Ward in a Pandemic" was a finalist for the 2020 Rattle Poetry Prize. They live in Northampton, Massachusetts, and are pursuing a PhD in botany at University of Massachusetts Amherst.

Jennifer Clark is the author of a children's book and three full-length poetry collections. Her newest book, *Kissing the World Goodbye* (Unsolicited Press, 2022), ventures into the world of memoir, braiding family tales with recipes. She lives in Kalamazoo, Michigan. Her website is jenniferclarkkzoo.com, and you can also find her on Instagram at @jenniferclarkbooks.

Marisa P. Clark is a queer writer whose prose and poetry appear in *Shenandoah, Cream City Review, Nimrod, Epiphany, Foglifter, Rust + Moth, Texas Review, Sundog Lit, Air/Light*, and elsewhere. *Best American Essays 2011* recognized her creative nonfiction among its notable essays. A fiction reader for *New England Review*, she hails from the South and lives in the Southwest with three parrots, two dogs, and whatever wildlife and strays stop to visit.

Eve Croskery is a writer, mother, and primary school teacher. She lives in Auckland, New Zealand, with her partner and two young children, who have helped her to rediscover her creativity and passion for writing. You can read more of her work on Instagram at @evepoetry_.

Jodie Duffy (she/her) lives in Gloucestershire with her husband and daughter. She is a Chinese studies graduate and works as a publications manager. Much of her poetry is inspired by motherhood and nature. Her poems can often be found in the notes app of her phone in between her shopping lists. You can read some of them on Instagram at @chrysanthemum_poetry.

Mary Clements Fisher relished careers as an educator and businesswoman and celebrates her current mother/grandmother, sweetheart, student, and writer status in Northern California. Writing makes sense of her mad and muddled moments. She's published in *Quail Bell Magazine, Adanna Literary Journal, Passager Journal, The Weekly Avocet #450, Personal Sto-*

ry Publishing Project, Prometheus Dreaming, and *The Closed Eye Open.* Join her on Instagram at @maryfisherwrites and on her website maryfisherwrites.squarespace.com.

Isabel Glass (she/her) is a healthcare worker from Massachusetts. As a graduate of Middlebury College, she spends much of her time dreaming of Vermont Octobers. Isabel also loves struggling through Sunday crosswords, running with her rescue dog, Phoebe, and listening to rainfall. "Dental Records" is her first published piece.

Aiden Heung (he/they) is a Chinese poet born in a Tibetan Autonomous Town, currently living in Shanghai. He is a Tongji University graduate. His poems written in English have appeared in *Australian Poetry Journal, The Missouri Review, The Orison Anthology, Parentheses, Crazyhorse,* and *Black Warrior Review,* among other places. He also translates poetry from Chinese to English, and his translations were recently published in *Columbia Journal* and *Cordite Poetry Review.* He can be found on Twitter at @aidenheung.

Paul Hostovsky's latest book of poems is *Mostly* (FutureCycle Press, 2021). His poems have won a Pushcart Prize and two Best of the Net awards and have been featured on *Poetry Daily, Verse Daily,* and *The Writer's Almanac.* You can find him online at paulhostovsky.com.

Nancy Huggett is a settler descendant who lives, writes, and caregives in Ottawa, Canada, on the unceded territory of the Algonquin Anishinaabeg people. Thanks to Firefly Creative, Merritt Writers, and not the rodeo poets, she has work out or forthcoming in *Citron Review, Five Minute Lit, Intima,*

Literary Mama, One Art, Pangyrus, Prairie Fire, (Re) An Ideas Journal, and *Waterwheel Review.*

Anna Kibbey is a food copywriter, journalist, and poet living in London with her current husband and children. Her work has appeared in the *Evening Standard* and *Between the Lines.* You can find more of her poetry on Instagram at @by_annakibbey.

Gita Labrador (she/her) writes from the Philippines. You can find her work in *Honey Literary, FERAL, Glass, Scum Mag,* and elsewhere. She lives in Quezon City, where she teaches high school English and tries her best to keep her houseplants alive.

Cynthia Landesberg was born in Busan, South Korea, adopted by Jewish parents, and grew up in the suburbs of Washington, DC, where she still resides. She is a mother, lawyer, and writer. You can find more of her writing in the *Washington Post* and *Witness Magazine* and on her website adoptionsquared.com.

Emerald Liu is the poetry and prose editor at *Asians in the Arts* and poetry editor at *Kluger Hans.* Her debut poetry chapbook, *Double Happiness,* was published by birdbeakbeast press. She was selected to attend the Paris writer's residency of deBuren this summer.

Joan Mazza has worked as a medical microbiologist and psychotherapist and taught workshops on understanding dreams and nightmares. She is the author of six self-help books, including *Dreaming Your Real Self* (Penguin Putnam). Her poetry has appeared in *The MacGuffin, Valparaiso Poetry Review, Prairie Schooner, Adanna Literary Journal, Poet Lore,* and *The Nation.* She lives in rural central Virginia.

Mary McColley is a writer and poet originally from Maine. She lived and wandered around Paris, France, for a number of years, and is working at the moment in Thailand. Mary is fascinated by languages and migrations; she loves running, art, and the sea. Her work has appeared in the *Paris/Atlantic* literary journal, *Maine Magazine*, multiple anthologies of the *Telling Room*, and on public radio broadcasts. She authored the mystery novel *A Wrinkle in Crime* and occasionally boils lobsters.

Shaun Anthony McMichael has taught writing to students from around the world in classrooms, juvenile detention halls, mental health treatment centers, and homeless youth drop-ins throughout the Seattle area. Over fifty-five of his works have appeared in literary magazines, online, and in print. He lives in West Seattle with his wife of over ten years and his son with special needs.

Veronica Nation (she/her/hers) is a Colorado poet and artist whose work has been featured in *Capsule Stories, The Allegheny Review, 300 Days of Sun,* and other literary journals. In her spare time, Veronica enjoys drinking iced coffee, immersing herself in yellow, and taking pictures of things she loves. You can read her writing on her website at veronicanation.com and on Instagram at @rainandpoetry.

Sam Neboschizkij is a writer and filmmaker based in Montréal, Québec. Her work gravitates toward exploring the interior lives of women, experiences of becoming, and liberation struggles large and small.

Katherine D. Perry is a professor of English at Perimeter College of Georgia State University, where she teaches writing and American literature. Her first book of poetry, *Long Alabama Summer*, was released in December 2017 by Finishing Line Press and draws heavily on her childhood experiences of growing up on the Alabama Gulf Coast. Her poems have been published in journals such as *Fresh Words*, *Writers Resist*, *The Dead Mule School of Southern Literature*, *Poetry Quarterly*, *Southern Women's Review*, *Bloodroot*, *Borderlands*, *Women's Studies Quarterly*, and *13th Moon*. She is also the cofounder of the Georgia State University Prison Education Project, which brings college courses to incarcerated students in Georgia prisons. She lives in Decatur, Georgia, with her spouse and two children and identifies as a Southern writer, even when that label is complicated. Her website is katherinedperry.com.

Taylor Stanton works as a content marketer in Springfield, Missouri. She studied English and creative writing as an undergraduate at Drury University and was once called a copy wizard. She tries very hard not to kill her houseplants and has a loud laugh. Seriously, you can recognize her by this happy cackle.

Emma Thom is a graduate of Sweet Briar College with a BA in English and creative writing. She received her master's in secondary education from Vanderbilt University and teaches English in New Mexico. Although she enjoys living in the Midwest, she continues to reflect on her East Coast upbringing through her short fiction pieces.

Ann Weil is a retired professor who lives in Ann Arbor, Michigan, and Key West, Florida. Her poetry can be read or is forthcoming in *Crab Creek Review*, *Whale Road Review*, *The Indianapolis Review*, *Third Wednesday*, *Eastern Iowa Review*, *Shooter Literary Magazine*, *Halfway Down the Stairs*, and *San Pedro River Review*. She earned her doctorate from the University of Michigan and writes poetry for obvious reasons: glory and big bucks. Visit annweilpoetry.com for more information.

Kim Weldin is a writer living in Charleston, South Carolina. She earned her BA in English from College of Charleston. Her work has appeared or is forthcoming in *Maudlin House*, *3Elements Literary Review*, and *Apple in the Dark*. You can find her on Twitter at @WeldinKim.

Editorial Staff

Natasha Lioe, Founder

Natasha Lioe graduated with a BA in narrative studies from University of Southern California. She's always had an affinity for words and stories and emotions. Her work has appeared in *Adsum Literary Magazine*, and she won the Edward B. Moses Creative Writing Competition in 2016. Her greatest strength is finding and focusing the pathos in an otherwise cold world, and she hopes to help humans tell their unique, compelling stories.

Carolina VonKampen, Publisher and Editor in Chief

Carolina VonKampen graduated with a BA in English and history and completed the University of Chicago's editing certificate program. She is available for hire as a freelance copyeditor and book designer. For more information on her freelance work, visit carolinavonkampen.com. Her writing has appeared in *So to Speak*'s blog, *FIVE:2:ONE*'s #thesideshow, *Moonchild Magazine*, and *Déraciné Magazine*. Her short story "Logan Paul Is Dead" was nominated by *Dream Pop Journal* for the 2018 Best of the Net. She tweets about editing at @carolinamarie_v and talks about books she's reading on Instagram at @carolinamariereads.

Claire Taylor, Editor

Claire Taylor is a writer in Baltimore, Maryland, where she lives with her husband, son, a bossy old cat, and an anxious dog who longs to be the cat's best friend. Claire's writing has appeared in a variety of publications, and she was a finalist for the 2020 Lascaux Prize in Poetry and winner of the 2021 *Serotonin* New Year's Day poetry competition. Her micro-chapbook, *A History of Rats*, is available from Ghost City Press. Claire is the founder and editor in chief of *Little Thoughts Press*, a print literary magazine of writing for and by kids. Claire joined *Capsule Stories* as a reader in March 2021. A selection of Claire's work is available online at clairemtaylor.com.

BEE LB, Reader

BEE LB is an array of letters, bound to impulse; they are a writer creating delicate connections. they have called any number of places home; currently, a single yellow wall in Michigan. they are currently working on two poetry manuscripts, *HEART GROTESQUE* and *SWALLOW THE TRUTH, COUGH UP BOTH HALVES*. they have been published in *Revolute Lit*, *Red Weather*, *opia*, *Capsule Stories*, *Catchwater Magazine*, and *Ample Remains*, among others. they joined *Capsule Stories* as a reader in January 2022. their portfolio can be found at twinbrights.carrd.co.

Aimee Brooks, Reader

Aimee Brooks (she/her) is a writer from West Texas making her way in the Pacific Northwest. She is attending Eastern Washington's MFA program to hone her skills and immerse herself in a community of writers. When she's not sitting at her desk, cup of coffee in hand, she's exploring trails with her husband, picking berries, and trying to train her cat to walk on a leash. You can find more of Aimee's work in *Goats Milk Magazine*, *Embers* literary magazine, and The Storytelling Project. Follow her bookstagram at @bookie.of.the.year.

Stephanie Coley, Reader

Stephanie Coley is a country girl from Gering, Nebraska. She graduated in 2016 from Concordia University, Nebraska with a BA in English and a minor in art. She has been a journalism teacher, janitor, data technician, and more. Stephanie is a published poet, appearing in the National Creativity Series of 2009 and *Mango* Issue 3, Respeto, in 2017. She is also a winner of the 2020 Historic Posters Reimagined Project, which can be found at the Nebraska History Museum in Lincoln, Nebraska. Stephanie currently works as the program manager at the West Nebraska Arts Center in Scottsbluff, Nebraska. Stephanie joined *Capsule Stories* as a reader in January 2021.

Rhea Dhanbhoora, Reader

Rhea Dhanbhoora worked for close to a decade as an editor and writer before quitting her job and moving to New York to get her master's degree and finally writing the stories everyone told her no one would ever read. Her debut poetry collection, *Sandalwood-Scented Skeletons*, was published by Finishing Line Press in 2022. Her work has appeared or is forthcoming in publications such as *Sparkle & Blink*, *Awakened Voices*, *Five on the Fifth*, *Capsule Stories Autumn 2020 Edition*, *Fly on the Wall Press*, *HerStry*, *Artsy*, *Broccoli Mag*, and *JMWW*. Her work has been nominated for a Pushcart Prize and Best American Essays. She is currently on the board of directors for the literary organization Quiet Lightning and editor of RealBrownTalk. Rhea joined *Capsule Stories* as a reader in January 2021. She's working on several projects, including a linked story collection about women based in the underrepresented Parsi Zoroastrian diaspora. You can read her work online at rheadhanbhoora.com.

Hannah Fortna, Reader

Hannah Fortna graduated in 2016 from Concordia University, Nebraska, combining her passion for the written word and her affinity for art making with a degree in English and a minor in photography. After a three-year career as a freelance copyeditor, she heard traveling calling her name and now works seasonal jobs in places connected to America's national parks. When she's not selling souvenirs to tourists in gift shops, she enjoys hiking, photographing natural spaces, and writing about the flora and fauna she saw while on the trail. She reads anything from poetry to middle-grade novels, but the nature-inspired creative nonfiction section is her haunt in any bookstore. Her poetry has previously appeared in *Moonchild Magazine* and *Capsule Stories Spring 2019 Edition*. Hannah joined *Capsule Stories* as a reader in November 2020.

Teya Hollier, Reader

Teya Hollier is a graduate of York University with a BA in creative writing. At York, she won both the Babs Burggraf Award and the Judith Eve Gewurtz award for her poetry and prose. Her work has previously appeared in *Room* magazine, *Verses Magazine*, *OyeDrum Magazine*, and *Capsule Stories Second Isolation Edition*, where she was nominated for a Pushcart Prize. Teya joined *Capsule Stories* as a reader in January 2022. When she is not writing, she is reading and reviewing books, watching horror movies, drinking copious amounts of tea, and bingeing *The Great British Bake Off*. She is currently working on a collection of short stories and a ghostly novella.

Mel Lake, Reader

Mel (Melodie) Lake is a writer and editor who lives in Denver with her partner and a very good dog. She received an English BA from Northern Arizona University and an MS in technical communication from Northeastern University. Her essays have been published in *The Mark Literary Review* and *Capsule Stories* and her fiction in various places including *Stratum Press* and *Land beyond the World*. The full list of her publications can be found at mel-lake.com. She's working on a novel, is a comics nerd, and always forgets to tweet at @melofsometrades. Mel joined *Capsule Stories* as a reader in January 2022.

Kendra Nuttall, Reader

Kendra Nuttall is a copywriter by day and poet by night. She has a BA in English with an emphasis in creative writing from Utah Valley University. Her work has previously appeared in *Spectrum*, *Capsule Stories*, *Chiron Review*, and *What Rough Beast*, as well as various other journals and anthologies. She is the author of the poetry collection *A Statistical Study of Randomness* (Finishing Line Press, 2021) and *Our Bones Ache Together* (FlowerSong Press, forthcoming). Kendra lives in Utah with her husband and poodle. When she's not writing, you can find her hiking, watching reality TV, or attempting to pet every animal she sees. You can find out more about her work at kendranuttall.com. Kendra joined *Capsule Stories* as a reader in January 2021.

Rachel Skelton, Reader

Rachel Skelton graduated from William Woods University with a BA in English, a concentration in writing, and a secondary major in business administration, a concentration in management. She has interned for Dzanc Books and now works as a freelance fiction editor specializing in speculative fiction. You can find more information about her work at theeditingskeleton.com. She occasionally tweets about editing at @EditingSkeleton and talks about books she's reading at @TheReadingSkeleton on Instagram. When she's not doing anything reading-related, she's hanging out with her cats, collecting houseplants, and attempting to learn how to crochet. Rachel joined *Capsule Stories* as a reader in January 2021.

Deanne Sleet, Reader

Deanne Sleet is a graduate of Saint Louis University with a BA in English, a concentration in creative writing, and minors in African American studies and women's and gender studies. She has interned for *River Styx* and Midwest Artist Project Services, where she gained experience with grant writing, editing, and writing copy. She is currently the leasing and marketing manager at City Lofts on Laclede and holds the secretary position for SLU's Black Alumni Association. She writes short fiction and poetry, and a novel is in the making. In her spare time, she hangs out with her cat and roller-skates. Deanne joined *Capsule Stories* as a reader in February 2021.

Annie Powell Stone, Reader

Annie Powell Stone (she/her) is a fan of peanut butter toast. Poetry recently came back to her after many years away and has absolutely saved her sanity during lockdown. Her work has appeared in *Door Is a Jar*, among others. Her published poetry can be found in her online portfolio at https://5fd9df8032a50.site123.me/. She joined *Capsule Stories* as a reader in March 2022. Annie got her BA in English from the University of Maryland and her MS in education from the University of Pennsylvania. She is currently pursuing accreditation from the Orton-Gillingham Academy for her work as a reading specialist with kids. She lives on the ancestral land of the Piscataway people with her husband and two kiddos in Baltimore City, Maryland, where she proudly holds the post of Front Desk Lady at a small K–8 school. Read more of her poetry on Instagram at @anniepowellstone.

Emily Uduwana, Reader

Emily Uduwana (she/her) is a poet and short fiction author based in California. She received her BA in history from CSU Northridge and her MA in history from UC Riverside, where she focused on queerness, gender, and sexuality in early California. Her work can be found on her website and in publications like *FUNGI Magazine*, *Stonecoast Review*, and *Capsule Stories Autumn 2021 Edition*. Her debut poetry chapbooks, *Knotted* and *An Expedition to the Desert of Andromeda*, were released in 2020 by orangeapplepress and Roaring Junior Press. Her next chapbook and first collection are forthcoming from Louisiana Literature Press and Nightingale & Sparrow Press in 2022. Emily joined *Capsule Stories* as a reader in January 2022.

Amy Wang, Reader

Amy Wang is a student from California. Her work has been recognized by the Scholastic Art and Writing Awards, the YoungArts Foundation, and Columbia College Chicago, among others. In her free time, you can find her crying over fanfiction or translating Chinese literature. Amy joined *Capsule Stories* as a reader in January 2022.

Submission
Guidelines

Capsule Stories **is a print literary magazine** published once every season. Our first issue was published on March 1, 2019, and we accept submissions year-round.

Become published in a literary magazine run by like-minded people. We have a penchant for pretty words, an affinity to the melancholy, and an undeniably time-ful aura. We believe that stories exist in a specific moment, and that that moment is what makes those stories unique.

What we're really looking for are stories that can touch the heart. Stories that come from the heart. Stories about love, identity, the self, the world, the human condition. Stories that show what living in this world as the human you are is like.

We accept short stories, poems, and remarkably written essays. For short stories and essays, we're interested in pieces under 3,000 words. You may include up to five poems in a single poetry submission (please send them all in one Word document), and only send one story or essay at a time. Please send previously unpublished work only ("published" includes pieces that have been posted or made publicly available on a blog, website, or social media platform). You may only submit one submission per edition. Simultaneous submissions are okay, but please let us know if your submission is accepted elsewhere. Please include a brief third-person bio with your submission, and attach your submissions in a Word document (no PDFs unless your poetry has very specific formatting, please!).

Find our full submission guidelines and current theme descriptions at capsulestories.com/submissions.

Connect with us!
capsulestories.com
@CapsuleStories on Twitter and Facebook
@CapsuleStoriesMag on Instagram

www.ingramcontent.com/pod-product-compliance
Lightning Source LLC
Chambersburg PA
CBHW040533170726
48295CB00012B/447